NAKADAI

A NOVEL

by

WALKER ZUPP

MONTAG

First Montag Press E-Book and Paperback Original Edition August 2022

Montag Press ISBN: 978-1-957010-14-4
Design © 2022 Amit Dey

Montag Press Team:

Cover: Rick Febre
Cover Photo: Photographer Unknown, Full Copyright W.Zupp.
Author Photo: Ellie Moore
Editor: Charlie Franco
Managing Director: Charlie Franco

A Montag Press Book
www.montagpress.com
Montag Press
777 Morton Street, Unit B
San Francisco CA 94129 USA

Printed & Digitally Originated in the United States of America
10 9 8 7 6 5 4 3 2 1

"After *Martha*, his extraordinary debut, Walker Zupp does it again with *Nakadai*, set in an almost recognisable alternative universe in which questions of language, theology, music and philosophy coalesce around accounts of the life of the central character, all haunted by the ghosts of God and a certain Austrian philosopher. *Nakadai* is strange, erudite and above all, hilarious."

– **Charlie Gere,**
Professor of Media Theory and
History at Lancaster University.

"By turns brilliant and knowingly absurd."

– **Stephen Gallagher,**
author of *The Authentic William James.*

"Kurt Vonnegut meets Ann Quin meets Douglas Adams."

– **Rob Magnuson Smith,** author of *Scorper.*

"*Nakadai* has some structural affinity with Nabokov's *Pale Fire*, but from there it hurtles back to the likes of Burroughs and Kotzwinkle as well as, more recently, Will Self, writers who - appropriately, given Nakadai's involvement in the purposes and mechanisms of language - are less interested in narrative than in the sentence and the idea, piling up the absurd and the epiphanic into a coruscating whole. It's an experience rather than a story, challenging and provocative throughout, and perhaps a little mad too. Buckle up and dive in."

– **George Green,** author of *Hawk.*

"Bizarre and compassionate. If life regularly confuses you, read this book."

– **James Bone,**
writer of *Laura and Peace.*

"One can picture Walker Zupp's sly grin as he composes *Nakadai,* an absurdist fantasy narrated by a grad student where a philosophical genius is empowered and enslaved by an inter-dimensional being called the Great Word who plots to invade the world. Written with breathtaking pace, language, academics, and eastern and western civilization are skewered by Zupp's rapier wit. Zupp captures the pathos and absurdity of contemporary life as his prose propels the reader into a parallel world that often feels eerily like our own."

– **Stephen Scott Whitaker,**
National Book Critics Circle

TABLE OF CONTENTS

DEDICATION

For Ellie, who's better than Wittgenstein.

ACKNOWLEDGEMENTS

I would like to thank Nigel Pleasants, Alessandra Tanesini and John Hyman for their conversations on Ludwig Wittgenstein. I'd also like to thank the British Wittgenstein Society for the interesting conversations they've facilitated through their Facebook group.

I would like to thank Rob Magnuson Smith and Jason Baskin for advising me throughout my doctorate.

I would also like to thank Naya Tsentorou and Natalie Pollard for their kindness; as well as Maddy Oliver, Emily Bernard, Georgia Taylor, Bevan Hewson and Ally Cotterill for their charity and conversation in Falmouth's Picnic Café.

I would like to thank Charlie Gere, Stephen Gallagher, George Green, James Bone and Stephen Scott Whitaker for reading my manuscript. I would like to thank Gabriel Boyer for being such a good editor outside of this process; and for keeping me company.

I would also like to thank Jason Hall for lending me his office, in which a great deal of writing was done. I wish to thank Truro Imagery for scanning Franco's slides so that we could have that wonderful cover; and double-thanks to Rick Febre for *making* that wonderful cover!

I wish to thank those at Montag Press, and my editor Charlie Franco, who have published this work—as always, they have helped to realize my ambitions for the book.

1

NARRATOR—GENIUS

I start my mornings by listening to Mozart's *Hunt Quartet*—a string quartet whose opening movement features a motif mimicking a hunting horn. I shower slowly, dress soberly and eat a fastidious breakfast of cherry scones and black coffee. I then sit at the picnic desk I purchased from Homebase and start work.

My work today is somewhat different, however. Today I intend to document the history of Hiroshi Nakadai, Professor of Neo-Linguistics at the University of Twickley who, only recently, ceased to be my tutor. I submitted my PhD in Theoretical & Applied Linguistics yesterday morning, then sat down and cried to the *Hunt Quartet* as though I'd taken centre-stage in some dreadful campus comedy. Be warned, reader: I do not intend to offer such frivolity *this* morning.

Taking up any lengthy residence in an academic department is like all that *free-form jazz* pioneered by Ornette Coleman and John Coltrane: complex improvisations on a single theme with a predilection towards the atonal which increases with each passing day. I'm not entirely sure why I decided to *do* a PhD—so, let it be known that I, Nicola Hillam-Joiner, have absolutely zero intention of embarking on any kind of academic career. I don't want to be part of any research institution. I don't want their concrete and plastic touching my skin. I don't want their scents of coffee and Lynx penetrating my nostrils. I don't want Stravinsky's *Oedipus Rex* battering my eardrums—my neighbour in the doctoral student office, who has every intention of becoming a tenured professor, has a habit of playing Stravinsky at full volume.

Nor do I want their administrative staff talking to me. I have been at the University of Twickley for 4 years now, and I have reached the *unpopular* conclusion that when you give men power, they get stupid and arrogant, and when you give women power, they become scheming and evil. Both conclusions are about as progressive as the social and cultural protest against urbanization you find in *punk rock*—and *neoclassicism*, to boot. But why, as Sid Vicious demonstrated so disastrously, do we *want* things to progress? For example, is nihilism progress? If their predilection toward swastikas is anything to go on, I don't think progress is necessarily enjoyable.

Human lives are *short* things. They can only be endured with an arcane mixture of pathetic values, ingratitude and anger. It's arcane because it works in life and the operas of *Pizzetti*. With that in mind, I would like to live my life with as little trouble as possible. I am sure many would say this indicated a non-life; the kind of pathetic existence melodically suggested by John Davy's organ compositions. I think the so-called glorious and effectual lives offered by solicitor's offices, investment firms and academic departments amount to Davy-esque existences—but my opinions are not going to save the world. (This got drummed into me when I started my doctorate.)

My grievances are my position in the universe. I will go to work on a Scottish farm when I finish writing Nakadai's story—preferably over the next 5 hours while I still have energy.

I am sitting in my one-bedroom apartment on Bashful Lane. (Down the road is where Nakadai used to live.) I own dangerous electric heaters because the *real* heating doesn't work. The shower takes ages to heat up and my water bill is high—but the gas oven is warm and the picnic desk I bought from Homebase is my best friend. "A friend should be a durable thing," Nakadai once told me. "That's why there are so few around."

It's July and bright outside. The wind blows through the window and cools my armpits; dries the sweat on my forehead.

Nakadai's parents were Japanese and were called Haru and Mari Hiroshi. They were both involved with the Japanese Olympic team; he, the official coach and she, a renowned sprinter. They decided to build their house in Gifu Prefecture where wood pigeons plumped through the warm air and where the earth was mostly fertile. It was not unlike *The Garden of Fand*, that tone poem by Arnold Bax whose mystical Irish mythology details the lifting of an island from the sea. Mari had designed the house with the attention a mother hen pays to fresh birdseed, which Haru really resented because he was a man and wanted always to be involved in the most practical of activities. But Haru—unlike the ideal Haru—was not a practical man but a *philosophical* man after whom his son would take almost completely.

> Acceptance is key. And I had to accept that I was exactly like my father. He was intelligent, arrogant and could focus relentlessly so that the world was unremembered.

The two-tiered, circular house was completed. The Hiroshis moved in and planted their first seed as though they had only recently pitched their tent at the Bath Festival. Evenings thereafter were exceedingly eerie and accompanied by Mari's piano ramblings. She was an accomplished pianist who arranged personal renditions of Ulysses Lachnér, Uwe Becker Smït and Anna Cläshna. Haru hated every one of these composers and much preferred Rachmaninov's *Aleko*—not that he was able to broadcast these musical tastes in any way. Thus, after dinner, Mari's methodical playing would fill the house with noise and Haru would sit on the Celtic-blue couch scribbling his ideas into a little notebook. One of the ideas he scribbled was:

> 8,000 bricks build one house; an additional brick completes the 8,000; therefore, the house is unfinished (re: is it a case of 7,999 or 8,001??? i.e., which side is the limit unfinished?)

But Haru could never straighten his paths or illuminate his alleyways of mind. The copious writings he would produce would never appear in public. They are hidden to this day like Thelonious Monk's unfinished brass symphony.

Every night, however, there would come a point when Mari's methodical playing irritated Haru to the extent that he'd throw down his pad of paper, jump off the couch, shout and point his finger at Mari and proceed in this fashion for about 10 minutes. "This happened every night," Nakadai recalled, "so it became a kind of cue." Mari would calmly leave the piano, tell Haru that she loved him, walk up the snail-shell stairs to the master bedroom and go to bed. This would send Haru into an even *bigger* rage where he'd stomp around the kitchen, throw his glass of water at the wall and scream and shout about marrying the wrong woman in Japanese and English. This would only last 30 minutes—then Haru, sufficiently calmed, would crawl up the snail-shell stairs and have passionate sex for what must have been the maximum amount of time, either in Japan or anywhere else. He was the temperamental equivalent of Animal from *The Muppets*—minus a drum kit, regrettably.

I can only relay what Nakadai has told me: as far as I can tell Nakadai was born in Gifu Prefecture on 18 November ——. It was around lunchtime, which for Japanese consist usually of bento boxes taken to work, although as Mari and Haru were at home, consisted that afternoon of ham sandwiches and miso soup. The baby Nakadai thereafter was welcomed into the family and was totally inept at sport, physical movement and breathing and therefore presented a strange familial counterpart to the annoyingly active Mari and the dull, drilling Haru. "But they never treated me any differently," said Nakadai. "They never worried about my inadequacies because I was their son." From the get-go, it appeared that he was gifted in other ways. Like Gustav Holst, he was remarkably intelligent and perceptive in just about every respect. He could listen to people as well as music, and the more he did this, the more determined he was to educate himself...

2

EDUCATION—MARI'S DEATH

Nakadai was certainly a type when it comes to academics: the wrapped-too-tight, dedicated-but-disliked, hard-working aristocrat of a thinker who students love but colleagues detest. Then there were others like my secondary tutor Dr. Goro Saito who kept on good terms with everybody, played the game to his advantage and managed to benefit the university financially. The American composer, George Crumb, had an eclectic style where Nakadai's notes and Saito's scales could have easily cohabited. They were both involved with my dwindling doctorate, and they had met one another *at* the University of Twickley during their research for *their* doctorates. They were cordial, but only inasmuch as Captain Beefheart and Frank Zappa were. But now, dear reader, I must recall Nakadai's earliest education which ran parallel to Mari Hiroshi's golden age as an Olympic sprinter.

Mari competed in the 100-metre dash at the North Korea Olympics and won gold, after which she saw Nakadai enrolled at Ureshino Nursery in Ginan via two economy-class plane tickets. He then attended Gifu Shiritsu Elementary School when he was 7—just after her triumphant silver-win at the Guam Olympics.

Mari subsequently led a poor campaign at the Gabon Olympics and blamed her performance on stomach pains. Despite these tummy-punches, she won bronze and saw Nakadai skip Junior High altogether and vomited on the plane back to Gabon.

I'd always been sceptical, weirded out whenever I heard that somebody had skipped a year (or several in Nakadai's case) as it came across as unnatural; maybe something his parents irritatingly encouraged. But Nakadai was always the arbiter of his destiny. Like Handels' *Music for the Royal Fireworks,* he seemed to live a life that had been scored for warlike instruments. It was during this time that his first serious development took place: Nakadai gave his first lecture at the Gifu Daiichi High School aged 14. What had happened was that he'd convinced the visual arts faculty to screen a "Sora Matsumoto movie masterpiece" called *Continental Nipple*.

> I was a boy. I didn't know Catholics flocked to the far east because they objected to the lack of religious freedom. I just thought they were bored. Much in the same way I'd no idea Sakamoto Sensei had developed *alcoholism*. I didn't know, for example, that were I to enable alcohol consumption it would turn me into a charlatan of the highest order, a seriously ticklish and controversial individual indeed. But that are things you do in the froggy days of youth that you would never attempt in the lonely years of adulthood: Saint Augustine was wild when he was young, and he got a corker of a book out of it. When you're that young, *a boy, as I was*, you don't know what evil consists of,

nor do you wish to entertain the idea that you *yourself* may have the potential for committing sin. That said, I wanted to screen *Continental Nipple* at my school; the only way I was going to do that was by bribing Sakamoto Sensei with alcohol. Because at 3 hours and 55 minutes *Continental Nipple* was as bad as the fact that in the years leading up to the bombing of Pearl Harbour meetings between Japanese officials and Catholic emissaries *increased*. As the events of Pearl Harbour, *Continental Nipple* was most regrettable. There's not much of a story *per se*: there's a man dressed up as a cow udder bulldozing all-girls boarding schools. In a manner of speaking the man wearing the cow udder had nothing of that self-scrutiny Catholic converts have for their former selves, praying for their Protestant friends to boot. The worst thing about the movie, in my opinion, was the music: orchestral extracts from *The Life and Death of Donald Glover* by Ulysses Lachner; far worse than even the most protracted German stumblings-of-faith.

It came as no surprise that Sakamoto Sensei vetoed the idea of showing Matsumoto's misogynistic musical brocade: a Zen-inspired monologue where he told me human life was but a flea on a hot griddle: no matter how high we jump, we return always to the searing metal where we arbitrarily contemplate our fate once more. Amid his quasi-soteriological ramblings, I yanked a bottle of vodka from my rucksack and placed the bottle in his shaking hands.

> Like a Japanese novelist cursed to wander Parisian streets, his eyes burned with the dichotomy of choice: the nearest Alcoholics Anonymous meeting or the bottle, the question churned in the clotted congealed mental cogs of his quite remarkable brain. He, unfortunately, chose the latter, unscrewed the top and started discussing venues. God did not choose me that day to be a messenger of peace but of *Continental Nipple*. The event ensued some weeks later. The film was screened and I went on stage afterwards and shouted, "*Hidoi*!" and this evil cackling erupted from Sakamoto Sensei in the back row, after which like a Catholic forced to recant his faith, he dragged his behind across the carpeted floor like a dog trying to remove an anthropomorphising pair of speedos. I tried ignoring him: I gave my thoughts on *Continental Nipple*, its merits and demerits, then fielded questions from my peers dodging filibustering burps from my evidently sloshed tutor, who, in his inebriation, reminded me that I had done an evil thing. Had the state made me do this? Where did my ethnic identity come from? How much should I rely upon culture: music, literature, religion? It's folly to think the state had no control over this. I considered Christ...

But a dark secret had been withheld from Nakadai whilst wowing his peers at Gifu Daiichi High School. Unbeknownst to the young Nakadai, his mother had been diagnosed with stage Two Invasive Epithelial Ovarian cancer and would die in under 2,000 days. In what was already a devastating series of events, his father made the disastrous, selfish decision to attend the Tibet Olympics with an improved Olympic Team, leaving Nakadai and Mari at home to foot the bill. The situation was *monothematic*, and Nakadai put to one side his education in the vain hope that doing this would improve his mother's health. He finished high school and returned home to take care of his mother, as it was clear that his father wanted nothing to do with either of them.

Naturally, or unnaturally, it was already too late. But in his spare time—for there are surpluses of seconds abound when the death of a family member is looming—Nakadai took to reading whatever he could get his hands on and developed a keen sense of self-education of which the numinous William Blake would have approved. Having imposed upon himself a lack of academic stimuli, he realized that he would have to not only design his syllabus but also teach himself—along with making the occasional ham sandwich for his mother.

His reading list consisted of English and French works that had been translated into English. He read Herbert Krim's *Radical Copying & Pasting: English Social Theory*, Tomas Verlitton's *The Hurried Imagination: A Brief History of Lippanángan Influence*, Yanis Moore's *Jacques Lippanánga: A Life of Compromise*, Joseph Becker's *The Science Fiction Audience and Their Mothers: The Case for a Genetic Obsession*, Terry Dyganty's *Science and Reaction and then Some*, Barbara Walters-Cox's *The Amateur and The Professional: Readers, Academics and Philosophers in the Twenty-First Century* and Virginia Jashpen's *The Feminist Victim and Other Ironies*.

The conclusion I drew from this reading list—considering that Nakadai was 15 at the time—was that whilst he had the conservative tastes of a young man, he simultaneously had a sense of his mind and was determined, inversely, to offend his pre-packaged sensibilities. There is always, as in Elisabeth Lutyen's Wittgensteinian *Motet*, the presentation of a challenge. We see Nakadai *challenging* himself with the work of Virginia Jashpen and Barbara Walters-Cox, as well as advancing an interest in the work of Jacques Lippanánga—a pivotal thinker in both his career and life.

Nakadai's mood, however, came to mirror the hostile Japanese winter. Mari's health worsened, and Nakadai understandably turned to fiction. Among such controversial works as Sue Takahashi's *The Woman in the Turtle*, Brionna Wecksnief's *Kill! Kill! Kill!* and Latanya Mandela's *Where The Dove Fell Flat and The Moon Flew Up*, there was, bizarrely, the short fiction of twentieth-century author H.P. Lovecraft, whose crazy tales of mythologized monsters and ghouls of lore—which, on occasion, resembled ethnic minorities such as Nakadai—he would but cherish in his early days, forgetting thereafter the pleasure he'd cultivated from reading Lovecraft's perplexing diatribes.

We now reach Nakadai's primary bookish influence: the Russian author and potter, Sergei Baryshev, whose gargantuan two-volume novel, *Pribislav's Sheath*, enthralled him with its quirky foreign perception of the world, colourful characters, ethno-philosophical explorations and overall moral purity. It was this moral purity that Nakadai obsessed over, reading the two-volume monstrosity many times over, memorizing whole passages by heart; sometimes wishing he inhabited the world of Ivan Pribislav and not the obfuscating, cognitive world of Hiroshi Nakadai.

> Unlike droll writers like Endō Shūsaku whose Christianity pulverized his literary dexterity, there are some authors, like Yasunari Kawabata or Latanya Mandela, whose words entertain and perplex you as Saint Augustine perplexed himself as he rampaged through Carthage drinking whatever he could get his hands on. What I mean is I began to imagine what my world would *sound* like had it been composed using *their* words. Not my own. One gloomy Saturday night I wrote a description of my world with words Sergei Baryshev would have used (*ideally*):
>
> "Mine was a time of *faith*. Faith brings not only silence but fear and noise to the heart. Mine was a time of *government*. Government brings not only place but felling and ruin to the state. Mine was a time of *character*. Character brings not only rarity but death and loss to the individual. Mine was a time of *heritage*. Heritage brings not only faith but apathy and upset to the family. Mine was an older time of faith, government, character and heritage. Mine was a time of green around the circular house, a time of fuzzy grass and thin sand substituting a higher verdant force. Mine was a time of woodpigeons, high-up clouds and cumulous and the shadow of mine father and the shadow of mine mother. Dastardly currents in mine time. For shame, I thought! Mine was but a quick preparation for the blue abyss of death..."

It is here, dear reader, that I must abandon my *bel canto* and sing the shattering demise of Nakadai's mother aged 38.

> Neo-Kantian moral relativism makes it impossible to judge someone else's actions as fundamentally morally wrong or unjust. In the same way, it's impossible for me to describe what it was like when my mother died, but what I *can* do is describe the event: I was worried about how I would pay for my mother's funeral, but she assured me everything was taken care of. Subsequently, the rule of death prevailed and I was left to carry out her wishes. I was 17 and was faced with the prospect of lowering my mother's corpse into a punt and pushing it out to sea. The history of Catholicism has shown how necessary education is in creating moral conscience, and the history of nearby Ibigawa fishermen had shown me they were the best men for the job. They may have had balding arachnid legs and jaundiced beards but they had huge hands and lowered me with my mother into the pre-selected punt of destiny. The youngest piscator, Kubozuka, knelt and said, "We'll be here when you get back, Nakadai-san." He untied the rope, threw it into the punt, and I started rowing down the blue, gooseneck thread to the Japanese sea. I thought about what Dostoyevsky said about modern socialism: how the modern atheist can more easily believe in Satan than God. When I came to, I had been rowing for an hour. I stopped rowing, watched the water around me, then looked

> at my mother swaddled like a child. Christ shows us the limits of science and individuals, I thought, so I picked her up and pushed her over the edge. There, in the queer bobbing of salted liquid, my mother sank. What makes my Catholicism hard work is how I believe, concurrently, that there is a lifeforce which embraces subject *and* object. This is why I don't have any pictures of my family. I can't imagine there is anyone, beyond those with brain damage or trauma, who needs a photograph to remember their mother...

Nakadai's father began to drink heavily and distanced himself from the son he had once cherished. Just as the shadows of his operatic contemporaries had forced Pacini into a provincial music school, the shadow of Haru's moral character, that abomination to humanity, inverted his soul and he went to live with his mother, Sakura, in Okinawa.

Nakadai, forever the arbiter, packed his bags and got in touch with a maternal aunt who lived in England. Ms. Chiba, as she was known to those lucky souls who entwined their life-weed with hers, was a petite woman with square hands, an oval-shaped face, a mouth full of blissful teeth and a high forehead that contained the greatest organizational mind in Twickley. Ferretti, that composer of light madrigals in Rome, would have called her a spinster. But she had *allowed* the Asian Supermarket she had founded to take over her life. Thus, Nakadai came to work at this establishment: that developmental part of our narrative that we now must turn to fearlessly...

3

KOTORI'S ASIAN SUPERMARKET —NAKADAI THE UNDERGRADUATE —DEUMON'S TALE

My problem with *The History of the Decline and Fall of the Roman Empire* is that it is too long. And any descriptions of the repetitive blur that Roman life consisted of would have doubtless stretched that already 6-volume work into 8 or 9 volumes—much in the same way, the character of Admiral Nelson forced Haydn's barking mind to generate the *Nelson Mass.* Wriggling my fingers away from any further digression, however: Twickley was a far cry from the past. Gone were the 3-storey terraced houses, freeze-dried pubs, lines of Alder- and Apple-Crab-Trees, basement clubs and bars. It was as though every landlord, owner and property developer had deemed current levels of literal construction to be inadequate. Thus, onto each triple-storied terraced house, another triple-storied house was built, and then another after that. Instead of the civilization (if you would be so callous to call Twickley civilization) creeping outwards like fungi, it stretched upwards into the sky. It became a very high city. Life seemed to dwindle at such heights. The most expensive flats touched the outer limits of the troposphere and were practically silent. At ground level, there were the persistent rattlings of the road-workers, street-salesmen, student protests and homeless people playing bongos. It was into this world of uppers, downers, cleaners, laughers and criers that Nakadai was thrown aged 17—Bach's debatably-named *English Suites* give a superior, phonic illustration of that world, in my view.

The first thing Ms. Chiba noticed about her little cousin was his exceptional English which would, she decided, be put to good use. Unlike other distant cousins, Ms. Chiba did not ask insensitive questions—but she did compel Nakadai to undertake phone duty at the front desk, the full account of which Nakadai shall now relay in full:

> I have observed a trend: a young person is forced to work menial jobs in the expectation that they will take their education seriously and work toward something worthwhile in their own time. I would tell Ms. Chiba how stupid this was: if I knew what I wanted to do (*which I did*) and wanted to work at it (*which I would*) then why should I spend my time doing frankly wasteful jobs like phone duty at the front desk? But Ms. Chiba would tell me to not talk so much and that I should work harder. I endured what must have been the shortest secretarial tenure

in the history of Chiba's Asian Supermarket and in the words of Saint Augustine: *it is time to confess, not to question.* The job was boring like *The Fortunes of Perkin Warbeck* and disturbing like *Inspector Miller and the Elasmobranch Banker.* I was totally inadequate, bad at being a secretary. I could not dream in the way that South Korean Presidents and Japanese Prime Ministers had dreamed about building a tunnel to link their two countries, an undoubtedly Catholic idea. A customer told me I sounded too smart to be working there. (Did they think I had dreams?) I had none of the power of religious women in Japan, their newfound Christianity bypassing priests altogether and bearing no resemblance to the patriarchal church found in Europe. I had no power and no dreams. I hated every customer who called up, their manners as bad as their grammar. I would turn red as they spoiled the English language and I would think about Christ. I would curse them and they would call back to re-ignite the argument. Then my wits would be at an end, my spirit shattered. I lasted a week in that job and finally Ms. Chiba permitted me to apply to the University of Twickley: Religion and Ethics (BA). Like a man who had converted from Protestantism to Catholicism, I felt as though I had come into port from a rough sea...

We can say then that at this point in our narrative Nakadai's course had been set from useless to useful. Nakadai was in no way a burden to Ms. Chiba, whose Asian Supermarket's shares recovered entirely after Nakadai's feisty tenure on phone duty had ended. Financially, he was independent of Ms. Chiba, as Nakadai had inherited a modest (adjusted for inflation) sum of £15,000,000 from his mother, and was more than capable of setting himself up with an apartment of his own—which, surprisingly, he did not do. He enjoyed the familiar tongue of Japanese at home and the bowls of *Goma-ae* Ms. Chiba prepared hastily in her shadowy, deep-fried kitchenette. Nakadai would play Nielsen's *Inextinguishable* Symphony on the stereo; a piece of music that sought to illustrate Nielsen's belief that despite our daily struggles all can be remedied by the power of music. (Not that Nakadai believed that.) He looked back upon these evening times most fondly, recalling the shrill depressing pattering of rain on the windowsill as Ms. Chiba's cooking filled the nearby distance of the very red apartment with happy aromas, happier memories and less than happy reminders of the life Nakadai had prepared for himself.

> Saint Francis was a curiosity in Japan: I felt the same in England. For me, however, returning to Japan was as likely as Francis returning to Spain. He died in China. And I knew I would die in England. I was exposed to things and people outside my country. And I rallied against my own. Formerly, the foreign figure of Christ had allowed Japan to reach out to the Vatican, then Italy. The local luminescence of England allowed me to see Japan more clearly. And England with less sympathy concurrently...

In September Nakadai was told he'd been allocated a room in student accommodation on campus not terribly far away from the Asian Supermarket. The buildings were seven-floored windowed rectangular prisms that had been painted a cheap coffee-cream colour that looked more like day-old crab meat than its name's butter-stained connotations suggested. Each room was an en-suite: a private toilet and shower available; the bed doubled as storage underneath and there was a desk that melted into the wall by way of a curved tabletop. It was a room of which the famed Mozart-interpreter, Karl Muck, would have approved. Indeed, the student architecture and design seemed to have been crafted by creepy, anti-aesthetic dentists in the primes of their careers. There were 7 rooms in each flat, with the rooms connected by a corridor that seemed to be out of Lovecraft's *The Whisperer in Darkness*. Nakadai seldom visited his room, preferring to live with Ms. Chiba, but once term started it became apparent that within that flat of colour-coordinated western students there was a brilliant mind which belonged to a young man called Deumon Belkacem. Nakadai's meeting him and their subsequent friendship had such an impact on Nakadai that he, in due course, subjected the disabled undergraduate to one of his now-infamous fictionalizations. In keeping with Nakadai's skewed but accurate depictions of reality, the tale of Deumon is a tragic one:

> Like a shopkeeper in one of Baryshev's novels, my life had erupted with misery. I was now an undergraduate at the University of Twickley where I lived in student halls. One of my flatmates was a boy named Deumōn,

who was the most grotesque human being I had ever met.

He took after the flightless parrots of New Zealand and was predominantly disabled. I never thought of him that way: I took Saint Augustine's line that everything could be doubted, that nothing could be certain.

I've always judged people on their soul and never their appearance. My parents were handsome people, but their souls were always what interested me.

In other words, a lot of physically-minded people disliked Deumōn because he was ugly. Whereas I liked Deumōn because I liked his soul—even if earlier I called him *grotesque*. There was no doubting his grotesquerie, but another word for grotesque is *whimsical*, which anywhere is a very good thing.

So, what was wrong with him? His head was a veiny, cyst-like dome that sloshed like a bottle of orange juice. And he had a motorized wheelchair that carried his feeble body around campus: there was no doubting he would pass through the mesh of scripture and find God.

One day he and I were sitting in his room. His bedsheets were the colour of dried blood and light shone through the double-glazed windows. I was sitting on his bed and he was in his wheelchair. "How do I know whether I'm evil?"

I tapped a pencil on my head. "Different belief systems have different cures. The good person's world is different from the evil person's world."

"*Life is a misery and I do not know when death may come.*" He paused. "Book Six, *Confessions.*"

"Buddhists think—though a Zen master would *deny* this because it suggests that duality between thinking and *not* thinking—it's quite natural to think you're evil. But if you're evil, and all your thoughts are *deceitful*, how can you trust your diagnosis? The problem is you can't. But it's no good saying, then, that you must be good. That would suggest the dualism between good and evil, and all kinds of dualistic thinking must be quashed if you have any intention of breaking free of *samsara*: the vicious circle of life and death."

"You're never going to reach Nirvana," he concluded.

I sighed. "There wouldn't be nearly as many problems if we spoke about this in Mandarin or Japanese. Where religion has trouble with diagnosis, language has trouble with precision. Then again what is precise for Ludwig Wittgenstein is imprecise for Jacques Derrida. What *is* precise for Derrida is the *impossibility* of precision. Wittgenstein thinks that's a load of nonsense, naturally."

Deumõn said nothing. His veiny, cyst-like dome sagged with contention. "As for us Catholics, we get original sin."

"There would've been a bar-room brawl if the author of *Genesis* knew about Aristotle's *prime mover* a few centuries later."

"Why?"

"The prime mover and original sin are extremely similar. The writer of *Genesis* has a problem: why does evil exist? They decide to account for it with an *original* sin, one that was so bad it set in motion every other sin ever."

"Except Aristotle widens the net."

"Exactly! He wonders why we're just talking about evil. Why don't we talk about everything: the whole universe?"

Hesitant to speak, Deumōn tapped his thin fingers. "I find myself wondering about the future more than ever."

"Whose future?"

"Mine." His eyes were like baptisms. "You won't always be here, Nakadai. You're a good man."

Deciding I might find something in the cheap flooring, I stared down for longer than I should have.

"It's unfair to burden people like I've burdened my mother."

"Tosh," I said. "Your mother loves you. Of course, she does. You can always see it in people's eyes."

"When Saint Augustine was in Carthage, he said he was in love with the idea of being in love. I don't see why parents and children can't have the same infection."

I listened to what he said. I thought he was bitter and he got worse over time. Near the end of term, he climbed out of his wheelchair, where the doctors had told him to stay, and crawled into bed. He pulled the dried-blood-coloured sheets over him and fell asleep. Then sometime in the night, he suffocated under the weight of his giant head and died.

His mother was called Janis and she collected his belongings from the housing block. Her face looked as though she had had something removed without anaesthetic and she looked right through me. Like when I had been talking about Derrida and Wittgenstein, she said nothing and calmly took what she could find.

No amount of thinking could have saved Deumōn. Thoughts and thinking cannot save *anyone* from themselves...

In the same way that the minuet in Haydn's *Clock Symphony* had been designed for a mechanical clock, Nakadai's developing brain had been designed to disagreeably, at that time, consider his remaining for an MA in Philosophy & Religion. He thought about the matter during a lunch of *Goma-ae* at the Asian Supermarket as he listened, once again, to Nielsen's *Inextinguishable* Symphony. The battling timpani backgrounded burly employees shifting boxes of dried squid; and Nakadai swiftly, amidst those swirling Danish strings, decided to email the only Liberian-Scottish woman in his department.

He asked Dr. Mairé Zeh Blah whether she wanted to supervise his MA dissertation, cheered privately when she accepted, finished eating his *Goma-ae* and undertook a nap at the back of the bustling warehouse where he dreamed a perfect word could describe everything and nothing simultaneously—Nielsen's strings and horns died out, and Nakadai's struggles were, that day, put to sleep by the power of music...

4

POSTGRADUATE—HARU'S DEATH—GORO SAITO

Zeh Bah was like Kurt Gödel and had a beyond-long-suffering wife who had a club foot and no sense of humour. For Nakadai, these were the details—but for his tutor, the details of Nakadai's MA thesis were rather more pressing and she coined the title *The Case for an Anti-Epistemology in Mardik Snül's On Linguistic Distinction* while he wasn't looking.

There are two things that are worth unpacking while my apartment isn't too cold and I'm not too low on calories. I'll put on some Fats Waller and get back to writing in two shakes of Waller's eyebrows...

Mardik Snül was a balding Polish man with a wonky eye who'd decreed to himself and two others—Stefanieb Yågosh and Jacques Lippanánga—that linguistics was dead and that the study of language ought to start again. Such was the motto of the Diacritics, a revolutionary trio of linguists who decided to ignore everything that had come before and thus create a Neo-Linguistics. (The Japanese composer, Yoritsune Matsudaira, undertook a similar route when inspired by established *gagaku* music, he decided to forge a modern classical sound with stones from the past and clouds from the future.) Mr. Snül—since he didn't have a PhD—was the oldest of the Diacritics and had worked for many years at the University of Columbia because (allegedly) he was so brilliant he didn't need anything beyond his bachelor's degree to prove he could work efficiently and brilliantly on a university faculty. (I am *not* in that echelon, unfortunately.)

Snül authored a paper called *On Linguistic Distinction* which did for linguists what Tchaikovsky did for Shakespeare enthusiasts: it made established texts even less intelligible and generally irritated everyone exponentially. The basic tenet of Snül's paper boiled down to the perfect word theory which as he liked to point out was better described as a hypothesis, but with the endless marketing the paper received was always labelled as a Theory.

Thus, the perfect word theory espoused the idea that there ought to be a word that simultaneously described everything and nothing, served every social function, performed every linguistic job imaginable and could be uttered once—never to be uttered again: the end of language. The only way to calculate this perfect word was through the construction of a Word Machine which over a prolonged period would calculate and produce this perfect word; and there would no longer be language and music, especially community singing, would have to be written into the constitution.

> I found freedom in the work of the Diacritics. It aligned closely to Japanese thinking, that is, the anthropology of Saint Paul. Unlike other writers, the Diacritics had a great belief in substance. The

> greatest belief belonged to Snül and his willingness to break language from substance. In doing so we would be able, finally, to focus on substance and not the language used to describe it. In the same way, Catholicism had a *progressive* potential in my country, the Diacritics had an *antagonistic* potential in the field of linguistics. After all, in doing away with language, you were doing away with rules. I have fond memories of those years when because I didn't know the rules, I couldn't break them.

I reminded Nakadai that you could still *break* a rule if you didn't know it—although Frank Zappa's compositions were most definitely the exception to this hypothesis.

> What made Snül antagonistic was his insistence that linguistic rules were wrong. Every one of them. He had a deep conviction that the universities were being eaten away by such rules. Not having a PhD himself, he pointed his finger at those who *did* and demonstrated religion *par excellence*: he had that *demand of the spirit* that sought his discipline, as well as the *intellectual self-satisfaction,* had in criticising that linguistic church in which he sermonized. For most people he was *Judas*.

Nakadai's MA, however, was in Philosophy & Religion and not linguistics. Thus, a trend again was set by the curious peculiar Nakadai; a credence that consisted of running at problems side-on and disregarding established methods, theories, individuals and choosing instead to bulldoze his way through the United Kingdom which he couldn't stand. As it happened, Nakadai wrote his MA thesis and dealt with the methods, validity and scope of knowledge in Mr. Snül's reviled masterwork, then thought a bit about God and considered deism and decided to apply for a PhD in Theoretical & Applied Linguistics. This was much to the shock and slightly irritated awe of Dr. Zeh Blah who spent subsequent rainy nights mulling Nakadai over as her club-footed wife enquired about what might constitute a quick divorce.

Unbeknownst to Nakadai—and thanks to a little creative journalism on my part—the Department of English Language & Linguistics had been paying attention to this peculiar Japanese boy in the Department of Philosophy, which, naturally, was separated from the Department of English Language & Linguistics by a bright orange door, behind which the Professor of Neo-Linguistics, Ellis Mutton, had been happily plotting for some time and watching Nakadai with an itching eye. He was a medium-sized fellow with diamondlike eyes, a thick shock of white hair that electrified his head in the sunlight and a small tummy that protruded most visibly whenever he turned regrettably to the side. He was the personification of the London Philharmonic Orchestra—and certainly *twice*, if not *three times*, as talented. On his deathbed Professor Mutton spoke with sable lips in Twickley Infirmary's Radiation Ward:

> All we're destroying are houses of cards. And Nakadai was most gifted in that respect. I had to have faith in something, not in my speculative intelligence, but

faith in *a man*. I lured him. Because he was quite extraordinary, a mature candidate, the most qualified I'd ever seen. He was on the verge of dropping out when I met him. I lured him. Stick it out, I told him. You'll see I'm right. And even as I lay dying *here*, in this stinking foreign place, I believe I'm vindicated, even if I'm not *contrite*...You've got to understand, Nicola, he rivalled every other student there. He had the ability to rival anyone he encountered, his intelligence and his perception, seemed to out-think and out-perceive, no matter the discipline, no matter the subject. Naturally, interdisciplinary prodigies irritate academics, I had to fight for him, tooth and nail. He was like something out of a book, a very long book: one of the first things he asked me was if I could get an appointment for him at the Russian embassy because he wanted to move to the country which produced that author of ludicrous tomes, *Sergei Baryshev*. I told him he was mad, but he persisted. I said he was potty, but he endeavoured to try and get citizenship. I'm not without influence in most places, Nicola, so I obliged Nakadai and got him a meeting at the Russian Embassy. They spoke about him unflatteringly and stamped REJECT on his application form. He was really sad about this; he thought his life was over. I told him that all good linguistic philosophy was about *saying only what could be said*—and this seemed to reinvigorate him. He wanted me to lobby for an ISMF-77/B North

> West Scholarship to fund his PhD—and the rest is history. Yes, *alas*, the rest is history...

Guido Cantelli was an exceptional musician who conducted music entirely from memory, and who died in an air crash. Putting to one side the unfortunate demise of this stellar individual, he was, like Ellis Mutton, considered to be The Shit in his respective field. Mutton had conquered the problems of the revisionist interpretation of the work language, Tonguetire. He had also brushed aside the onslaughts of Eighth Wave Feminism as personified by Queen Uliana of Algeria whose Berkeley-inspired line argued that words were merely concepts that didn't exist—a notion she also applied to men.

Mutton most notably, however, had written the comprehensive sequel to the original *Neo-Linguistics*: a twice-as-boring tome called *Principiis Lingua*. Was he friendly towards the awkward, arrogant, fascinating Nakadai? In many ways he was a father and provided solace where Nakadai had none; he would occasionally scold Nakadai for his ludicrous confidence, but never to the extent that Nakadai felt wronged or humiliated. He played the role John French had played against the domineering Captain Beefheart—Mutton was the mug that held Nakadai's creative coffee. He was the master of the gentle put-down and the king of almost silent praise which, when it came, seemed more valuable than all the precious un-conductive metals melted together into one expensive blob and valued according to its weight.

Nakadai began his PhD in Theoretical & Applied Linguistics aged 22. It is necessary to paint a picture of how this young adult appeared to the nervous, inquisitive colleagues who had the good fortune to encounter Nakadai before the vice-like grips of laboured aging gripped the man like a salamander in a child's petite clenched fist. Professor Duni Mwangangi gives on recollection:

> Of a somewhat greyish disposition with a snub nose, oval-shaped ears and a very small mouth at the sides of which already were tiny wrinkles. His eyes were feline and could, quite possibly, focus upon a single atom. His head of blackish hair was beautifully compact and easily trimmed. His thick expressive eyebrows, which would later thin with age, implied an unmistakeable thirst for observation.

Nakadai was Sir Peter Pears in search of Benjamin Britten: a most-talented tenor in search of operatic works in which that muscular voice of his would shake the thinker's world. But this young adult, so energetic and arrogant, so pious and dogmatic, would soon grow despondent and with sadness afflicted. There would be another death in the cursed Hiroshi family. It would be wrong of me as the author to assume that I could speak better of the emotional fallout of that death than Nakadai could himself—so I shall copy out a portion of Nakadai's own fictionalized version of the aftermath:

> Time is correspondent to space, and people are correspondent to time. As result people are never whole, they are incomplete.

What did it take for the Catholic Church to shed its traits as a foreign religion? There was a beach in Okinawa that shed its history and became timeless. Like the Catholic Church, it had seen many things. Things growing and dying, things appearing and disappearing.

What the beach saw was my father: Haru Hiroshi, struggling across the dunes, shotgun in hand.

He knelt in the sand and rested his chin on the barrel. He pulled the trigger with his toes and flew backwards.

Watching with delirious calmness, the beach saw police set up the forensic tent. They wandered around as children do on beaches.

Inspector Tsukuda peed on seaweed. He whipped his willy free of wee and zipped up his pants.

He walked inside the tent and found Sergeant Kimura stifling sickness. "Are you okay?"

The sergeant coughed. "Yea I'm fine." He looked away from the corpse and shook his head.

"You know he lived with his mother? Just up the hill, they were living. I can't blame him..." He frowned. "Let's go outside."

Tsukuda and Kimura strolled down the beach, their trench coats flapping like prayer flags.

"Isn't your dad Chinese?" Tsukuda asked.

"He's from Tibet. Why?"

"Just something you said the other day. Reminded me." He shrugged and watched their coats flapping in the wind. "There are no prayers here, for sure."

> "Agreed."
>
> The two policemen faded from history as did the death of Haru Hiroshi. And everything was incomplete...

Here endeth the tale—but this imagined aftermath, so restrained in its depiction, is redolent of only one thing: the fact that Haru Hiroshi (aged 52) committed suicide in Okinawa, after which his mother, Sakura, discovered the body picked at by gulls and fraternized by crabs. It was like *Bartolozzi* being cut down before penning *New Sounds for Woodwind*—or Chailly refused the chance to compose the operatic adaptation of Dostoyevsky's *The Idiot*. It showed Nakadai's family's decomposition in a stark depiction, and proved to Nakadai that should things continue in this vein, he would be the last of his species. Nakadai prepared himself for the doubtless fate that he believed would be spent solitarily under the overcast skies of Twickley which, in the manner exposed by Jarnach's completion of Busoni's *Doktor Faust*, forever reminded him that he did not belong.

> I think England is a country whose church is full but whose members all follow a different path in the world. The power of the individual is strong there and makes it hard to describe what it is like to live in England when you are *not* English. There is, too, a comparison with the United States. When I complain about England, I am also grateful that I *don't* live in America, and English people interpret this to mean England *is* progressive and open-minded. There is

> nothing progressive in England's heart. Like Sweden, a deep underlying conservatism affects everything: the *liberals* are conservative, the *activists* are conservative, the *artists* and *creatives* are conservative: a conservative utopia where petty anger is shrouded in serious garbs. The culture of *political representation* in America, for example, is more positive than in England. There is well-placed encouragement for people to run for congress in the United States. In contrast, running for parliament is looked upon with shame. When the member of parliament runs adrift, she is abandoned by everything on her travels. The church is indeed full, but its members each follow a different path in the world. The English experience is marked with shame and those who suffer the most are the English. But the church has its rules: it is always a shame that I am *not* English. When the social sciences fail me with their double standards, I well up with modesty and candour, and there is *nothing* I can't ignore...

Nakadai embarked upon a teaching course where, for the very first time, he would meet Goro Saito. He was a fellow Japanese from a vastly different background who would be Nakadai's oasis in this wasteland. PhD students from various backgrounds had been assembled to undergo training that would remind them never to yell at, sleep with or hastily punch undergraduates. Once there Nakadai got talking to Goro. He learned that Goro was the son of two Tokyo-based photographers who quite proudly didn't believe in God. He lived in the more affluent parts of Twickley, had furnished his apartment with carpets, paintings and mirrors and had celebrated wildly when he failed his first attempt at an upgrade. Nakadai reciprocally explained how his doctoral thesis would consist of analysing his MA thesis and how he was incredibly depressed because he had become part of an angry lopsided symbiosis which consisted of Nakadai and his MA thesis—which decidedly was dumb as hell.

Thus, Nakadai confessed for the first time his desire to commit suicide at 3:15 p.m. every day but without the shaming exercise of seppuku or hara-kiri. Doubtless, suicide was a predominant part of Japanese culture and Goro claimed, because of this, to understand what Nakadai was going through—but Nakadai grew angry and said that his wish to commit to suicide was not a cultural thing any more than it had been so for Socrates Androgathius, Cleopatra, Ryūnosuke Akutagawa, Sylvia Plath, Stefanieb Yågosh, Thaddeus Monkmill or his father, Haru.

Then with a tone that sounded like something out of a high note performed by Australian soprano Dame Nellie Melba, Nakadai summarized, "Unhappiness kills—*not* culture."

To say that Goro was struck by this would be an understatement. He was immensely aggrieved at Nakadai's loss, sought clarification, received it, cogitated privately upon what he had listened to for the past 5 minutes, and subsequently accompanied Nakadai out of the room when the teacher training had finished. It was there that Goro without warning hugged Nakadai very tightly and whispered in his ear, "*O-kuyami moushiagemasu.*" Goro's offering of his condolences brought Nakadai to tears. He thanked his fellow Japanese, lunched with him, partied with him and drank alcohol for the first time; then swore the next morning that he would never drink alcohol again and went about crafting his destiny with the trustworthy, knowledgeable Goro Saito at his weary side. Sir Peters Pears had finally found Benjamin Britten, and there would doubtless follow *Peter Grimes* and *Death in Venice* as well as countless other successful, intellectual recitals spawned from the energy of kindred spirits.

I remarked early on that Nakadai and Goro were cordial with one another—but in that glorious beginning, they were relentlessly comfortable with each other's company and were great friends. Their collective pebbles of time spent walking along the beach on Twickley's distant coastline, were like Thomas Morley's madrigals in his *Triumphs of Oriana*. Their shared innocence was rife and jolly as they walked along the beaches and observed the sometimes-rough water. They would plant their feet in the sand and stick out their arms, bracing themselves for the heavy winds which so often collided against Twickley's coastline. The wind would come and burn their huge smiles. Goro would enjoy these moments in near-silence. Whereas Nakadai would shout praises loudly at the sky and cry pleasure in the presence of nature's magnificence.

5

ARGUMENT—GOD—PHD

But those moments with Goro were anything but frequent. The architectural cesspool of Twickley turned from a beacon of hope to an emotional wasteland. The heavily stacked terraced housing, bongo-playing homeless people and the necessarily overrated presence of students on diesel-powered public transport began to get to Nakadai. With only one proposed year to go before Nakadai would submit his PhD for grading there was talk of his discarding the program. This understandably came to the attention of Nakadai's tutor, Professor Mutton, who was hopping mad at the prospect and demanded that Nakadai would remain until he had completed the program. Verily, Frederick Delius may have advanced from planting oranges in Florida to studying music in Leipzig—but he had received encouragement from Greig, and Nakadai suffered similar baiting from Professor Mutton. He said as much to me on his deathbed:

> Like a woman concerning herself with mathematics during a great war, I had my reasons for keeping

> Nakadai on. I'm sure you think that cabinet-making doesn't consist in glueing, Nicola, but that's irrelevant now. Everyone has secrets: Do you think Nakadai didn't? I've been ill my whole life, and the only respite I get is right now: a few painless hours following intense suffering...and the secrets die with me...

Professor Mutton exercised a considerable influence over Nakadai. The young PhD student grew anxious, overwrought, apprehensive and agitated; not unlike Benjamin Cooke, master of choristers at Westminster Abbey, on his very *worst* days.

For example, Nakadai came to be obsessed with adjusting the blinds in the shared postgraduate office. He would measure the light entering the room and gauge the appropriate angle for the blades, then rate the speed at which he would turn the adjustment stick and compute with staggering accuracy the forthcoming action. And Goro Saito, Garry Stathopoulos and Barrington Zapatero would survey these obsessive-compulsive happenings with growing unease. Saito would stir privately like one of *Longo*'s piano compositions; Stathopoulos would yawn as though he were a motif in Schubert's song cycle *Winterreise*; and Zapatero would chunter in a manner similar to *cantillation*, the chanting of holy scripture in Jewish worship. This would all go on and on until finally, Stathopoulos would explode yawnfully at Nakadai screaming, "Enough! That's enough! Stop adjusting the damn blinds! I can hardly think as it is!"

Nakadai came to resent his fellow PhD candidates as well as his tutor, Professor Mutton, who saw to it that Nakadai was caught always in the well-cast shadow of rare, linguistic beauty. So persistent was Professor Mutton's interest in the young Japanese; so obsessed and single-minded that he could not help but imagine a darker purpose that lent Professor Mutton his professional charisma and punctilious concentration. In a floating of words akin to the lyrics to *Londonderry Air*, there bubbled a series of questions to the surface.

> How old is Mutton? Where was he born? Why does he seem to know almost everything? And where does he get his energy from? People have been telling me about LSD. But maybe that's the cause.

With these queries mounting—as queries often do with PhD candidates, thus softening Nakadai's otherwise rock-solid nose for deception—Nakadai was convinced he would finish his degree and was instructed to visit Saint Xavier's Cathedral on the outskirts of Twickley. Once there, he would find a priest by the name of Father Brian Conner: a linguist-turned-priest who would shed light on Nakadai's less estimable worries and prove that Nakadai had nothing to worry about and ought to crack on with some work.

The contradiction was stark—if Nakadai should crack on with work, then surely his visiting some grammatical monk would be a waste of his otherwise valuable time, that is, time that needed to be spent doing the degree he had now set his mind on completing. He was like Bruno Maderna, that Italian composer who was so determined to experiment with performer freedom; but who was constrained by the technical limitations of electronic music of the time. This was most certainly *not* for Nakadai—not that Mutton agreed: "I'm sorry to hear about these depressing circumstances under which you're working," he told the sweaty PhD student. "You can't *want* to be a slumbering man aware of certain noises your *whole* life. Seek out Father Conner. He'll give a *proper* sonic introduction to the rest of your life..."

The fact of the matter was that Father Conner had studied linguistics at the University of Huddersfield. He had retired after 4 years in the service and lived the monastic life at Burton Abbey for 7 years, after which he became the rector at Saint Xavier's Cathedral in Twickley. It is not true that Father Conner was immediately present upon Nakadai's calling at the church, nor that Father Conner would happily clear up misgivings the young PhD student had. It appeared that before his appearance Father Conner had been left entirely out of the loop by Professor Mutton. What follows, admittedly, is far-fetched—PhD candidates like myself not being in the business of supporting far-fetched materials to appease any kind of reader—but, if it is genuine, then it should clear up the misgivings about Nakadai's past, present and future I had at that time.

> I followed Mutton's orders and travelled by bus to the centre of Twickley. I found Saint Xavier's Cathedral and stalked the grounds beset by snowbells.
>
> I worked up the courage to go inside and pushed myself through the narthex onto the nave. It was a dark,

cold place where I felt nothing but dread. Gradually I walked past towers, through the transept and stood opposite the pulpit. Father Brian Conner would stand there on Sundays and Thursdays delivering sermons to an ever-larger congregation.

Behind the pulpit, hanging on the wall, was a portrait of Jesus Christ. The portrait reminded me of how the European aristocracy declined during the 19th Century. The moneyed vapours of 7,000 land-owning families thronged in the dark and I felt pity for them, for Jesus Christ, for everyone and everything. It was like being in the 19th Century all over again—I would have started writing a novel about some derelict part of society, but I started crying and forgot about writing altogether.

I thought about my father and the miserable sanctum he had personified throughout our relationship. I was angry and disturbed, I kept crying because I was alone.

"I'm sorry!" I shouted at the portrait. "I'm sorry I snubbed him! There, I said it! I'm *so* sorry!" The uneven ancestral attitudes I harboured were suddenly level. Who cared if I fancied men? If logical inference broke down on a literary level, then the same was true for love: there was no logic in love, and love could not be contained.

I knelt on the lush, burgundy carpet where I wept and closed my eyes. When I re-opened them, an extraordinary change had taken place; English churches not lending themselves to *holy* transmogrification, anyway.

I looked up and found myself in a music video starring a half-talented rapper with perfect teeth—not literally, but it *felt* that way. The cathedral was a tinted stodge of rasping blackness. The room's configurations, ceilings and walls, were little more than vibrating outlines. And shapes floated around my teary visual spectrum.

Suddenly the door to the preparation room swung open. Father Brian Conner stumbled out like a badly-strung puppet. He spoke in someone else's voice: a powerful voice that seemed to think it was terribly funny. "It's a fine morning, tiny squid. How excellent to meet you in the flesh. Such...*lovely* flesh..."

I wiped my nose. "Who are you?"

"Professor Mutton knows me. That's not much of an answer, I know, but he sent you here, didn't he? To clear up a few things?"

Natural law may have been the best moral basis for a multi-ethnic country like Japan, but there was certainly nothing human about the ghastly apparition before me. Lovely space circled beneath my feet like massive bowls of ramen.

I was no stranger to psychedelic drugs. I had tried LSD to see if it would improve my powers of concentration. One of my *less* successful hypotheses, as it turned out.

Not having answered Father Conner's greeting, he sent my head into pandemonium. He pumped an awful screeching through my brain and laughed when I fell over. I drove my head into the carpet. "Stop it! You're hurting me!"

What replaced the screeching was a silence so deserted, so lifeless, that I regretted my outburst immediately. Meanwhile, the Orion Molecular Cloud had appeared above me.

"You don't like my singing?" Father Conner commented. "You've no taste. With parents like *yours,* I'm not surprised."

"Who—Who are you?"

The mouth thundered, "I am the *Great Word*. I have travelled great distances, *new* distances, to speak to you, tiny squid."

"I think you should go *back*."

"Don't be racist, tiny squid—"

"Shut up!"

"Be silent!" The cathedral vibrated with an alien power, very much like the Old Testament. "You cannot begin to understand the distances I have travelled. It is *beyond* measurement, it would make your head spin, now *shut up* and listen." A glaring blackness emanated from Father Conner's eyes. It encompassed the whole room. "In my company, you are a grain of sand; a single pebble among millions. But I'll cut straight to the point—"

"Thank you—"

"Shut up and stop talking!" The cathedral growled. "You are going to finish your doctorate. No matter the consequences, no matter the losses—you shall finish and continue your research."

The voice paused.

"*Please* stop crying, tiny squid. It is not the end of the world—not at current. And if it improves your mood, you were not my *first* choice. I am limited in this limiting reality of yours; I require a great deal of mental power—*their* mental power."

"Whose?"

"The first to serve me was *Francis Xavier*. He is a saint on this planet. But his fever did not improve his lack of intelligence. The second was *Ludwig Wittgenstein*. (You have odd names here.) He considered himself a philosopher. But his cancer did not generate humility inside him. I was the *most* impressed with *Stefanieb Yågosh*, the third. But the appetites she demonstrated reduced her to nothing. The finest mind on your planet, and now it is *gone*. Which brings me to you—"

"Professor Mutton!" I shouted back.

"*Who* and *where* Professor Mutton is, does not concern you, tiny squid! Human beings should not be in the habit of turning *simple* things into *complicated* things. Now, having said that, I shall build barriers in your mind. These will direct your thoughts to the right remedies, the right conclusions. When that is done, I shall release you."

There was an academic who said, that, despite their enthusiasm, the Japanese could never apply their beloved European literature to their own identity, and change.

In the Great Word's presence, I was in the same position. Its divine power impressed me. But would it change me?

I asked a reasonable question: "What do you want?"

"This may come across as *insincere*—but I *like* your planet, and—"

"You do?"

"I'm going to finish my sentence if it *kills* you."

"I—"

"What?"

"You call yourself the Great Word."

"It is a name like any other."

"But that must mean you're made of language—you're some kind of grammatical being! That's amazing!" I was lost in admiration. "Please, sir, I want to know *everything* about you!"

"You know nothing!" Again, the cathedral vibrated with an alien power. "When I look into your soul, tiny squid, I see that you are built from rules. These are useless. What you require is my will and you shall have it. Follow my instructions and you shall have vision, beyond all else, you shall have vision and sight and view. If you disobey me, I shall penalize you. I may *not* have a body, tiny squid, but

> I shall have an entrance. And you shall calculate its majesty—!"
>
> Then, like a scene from a B-grade *Exorcist* rip-off, Father Conner's body was de-possessed. He flew back onto the burgundy carpet in a shower of sparks and light.
>
> Father Conner regained consciousness shortly after and rubbed his head. "Communion wine...*must* stop drinking communion wine..." he muttered to himself. He looked toward the pulpit and saluted the portrait behind. "Aye, aye..."
>
> I ran out the cathedral and caught the bus back to campus. I caught Professor Mutton getting into his car and told him everything. He smiled when I told him how scared I was...

When I pressed Nakadai for further information he said: "All the information you need is in that piece of writing, so you should move forward with that and leave behind any additional fluff I could supplicate to those morose fantastical memoirs of mine." He refused to accept, however, that I was in Andrew Lloyd-Webber's position; that additional fluff was *precisely* what I needed!

When I first examined the preceding fictionalization, I was flabbergasted and retired to the sonic annals of my laptop for a psychological siesta. I listened to a series of nineteenth-century compositions written in the *Galant style*, that is, defined by elegant superficiality and ornamentation. My annoying doctoral neighbour entered the office and was disgusted by the superficial music which had been arranged by *Wagenseil* several centuries earlier. He coughed to get my attention and I ignored him. "Excuse me," he said.

"I can't hear you over the oboes," I replied.

"That's the problem," he complained.

"Not nice when it happens to *you*, is it?"

"The difference is I listen to good music—"

"The *difference* is you're a philistine." I returned to thinking about Nakadai's fictionalization. These were fragments and splinters of history. I couldn't make sense of them on my own. I pleaded with Nakadai, thereafter, to continue his remarkable story...

Thus, it should come as no surprise that Nakadai passed his PhD in Theoretical & Applied Linguistics with flying colours. The reasons as to why he did, however, remain bothersome and strange to Nakadai to no end.

Professor Mutton, Father Conner and the Great Word—everything was ripping to shreds Nakadai's insides. He did not look forward to the bondage-like employment his body and soul were set upon. But then something unexpected happened which threw everybody's plans off-kilter. It was like when Bertholt Brecht suddenly produced *The Threepenny Opera*; or when that anonymous idiot decided *cinema organs* should be played between showings.

In our case, it was a brain tumour. It was growing in the cerebral cortex of a certain high-powered South Korean General named General Chun-hei Choe. It got so big that it started to affect her mood and her ability to make decisions. Soon after, South Korea accused Japan of trying to invade their country through Tsushima Island, and this plunged both countries into a bloody conflict in which Nakadai, incredibly, would play a small part...

6

SOLDIER—DISCHARGE—SANATORIUM—ENGLAND

The word came from Germany; a Germanic base shared with the word "worse". Then through an Anglo-Norman French variant of "guerre" came the Old English word, "werre". Today the word is "war" and war is what we *have* (boast, retain, occupy). I have *declared* war; I am *at* war; I am *waging* war against the Great Word. I have gone to war (encounter, collision). I am going *to* war and will be *at* war. A war of attrition and words, for certain. *He trains my hands for* war *so that my arms can bend a bow of bronze—There he broke the flashing arrows, the shield, the sword, and the weapons of* war—*a time to love, and a time to hate; a time for war, and a time for peace*—the war to end all wars...

For a long time, Nakadai ruminated upon war—not realizing that the reality of war did not have much in common with the word "war".

War was a cold word like charity. And it was used by bureaucrats to justify their numbering human beings like Willem de Fesch numbered his violins. Thus, Japan's Nippon Progressive Government activated its *Emergency Powers Act* and the Japanese Recruitment Services were given the gift of Article 78/B: known colloquially as the Hara-kiri Bill because it reinstated a regime of mandatory 2-year military service for Japanese citizens between the ages of 20 and 30.

Nakadai was aged 27 and qualified. The choice may have been simple, but it was by no means easy. Either Professor Mutton could let Nakadai go to war and risk his life, or the newly certified Doctor of Theoretical & Applied Linguistics would go to a Japanese prison for a substantial amount of time and face beating and strangulation, weekly food reductions, being prevented from writing, reading, drawing and exercising and rules explaining how to sleep, where to look and how to stand. These were not the most promising prospects, so Nakadai was permitted to leave the University of Twickley on the damning condition that he would return to work thereafter serving his 2-year military service, which, as things turned out, would consist of active combat. He had committed to the *Carnival of the Animals*; and his lived experience would resemble, in many ways, that zoological fantasy in 14 movements by *Saint-Saëns*.

Nakadai was scared and nervous when he landed in Japan. He immediately delivered his draft card to the JRS Building in Tokyo, slept briefly on a bench, got on a coach, spoke to several of his fellow recruits—Kawaguchi, Yanagi, Iga and Omura—then flew to Okinawa for basic training at Kadena Air Force Base. His drill sergeant was a woman called Sergeant Tanaka who listened to the performances of Swedish soprano Birgit Nilsson incessantly. An important interpreter of Wagner, Nilsson sparkling renditions accompanied Nakadai's first experience with an AR-15 rifle and his scuttling up an army-issue jungle gym at Sergeant Tanaka's shouted request. Nakadai endured three weeks of Nilsson and barely slept. He would sometimes speak to Yanagi and Iga about modern-day Japan and listened to Omura and Kawaguchi talk about pussy and beer, or so they referred to as their weekends. Doubtless, Nilsson's overwrought *Brunhilde* would only have approved at gunpoint...

> Can be both a cat or a woman's genitals; also a term for plural femininity (womanhood, womanliness). There is then the *North American informal* meaning: a feeble, pigeon-hearted, mincing man. I feel (believe, fancy) many would call me this [...] As for beer, it is related to the Dutch "bier" and the German "*Bier*". It comes, however, from the *monastic Latin passive verb*, "biber," and the active verb, "bibere" [...] *And Jotham ran away and fled and went to Beer and lived there, because of Abimelech his brother...*

When he wasn't writing in his diary he dreamt about Ms. Chiba. He was not looking forward to his return to Twickley. The only thing he feared more was the day when he, Hiroshi Nakadai, would be instructed to get in a helicopter and prepare himself for battle.

One day he awoke and was told he was going into battle. (The diary entry for that day reads, "Oh dear....") The fresh wave of soldiers hopped into a fleet of CH-47 Chinook helicopters and flew across a significant amount of ocean.

> The helicopter next to us blew up scattering shrapnel everywhere. I could see through the window the helmeted heads bobbing inside. The helicopter sunk through the air and plunged into the water below. At that moment I remembered the Catholic Church had always been the same church. What changed, however, was how we went about assembling the Kingdom of God—I thought the same about war, and soon found myself praying to almighty God that I and my platoon would make it through unharmed. Miraculously our helicopter was unharmed and landed on Tsushima Island. We ran out of the helicopter like crazy people. "Get in the trees!" said somebody next to me. "Get in the trees!" The towering Omura who, like Gideon, could have led anybody into battle, was shot down. We couldn't bring him with us, we had to leave the body. Disembarking the landing zone the survivors ran into the foliage and found some solace under the twinkling, hot canopy. Sicne Omura was our platoon leader, we had to quickly elect another. They voted for me because they said I had the most *common sense*. However, looking back, that was the worst decision they made as I turned out to be a *tyrant*...

A week later Nakadai was perched on an ammo box in the Japanese camp playing cards with Yanagi, Iga and Kawaguchi.

Sergeant Tanaka and her incessant Nilsson recordings were nowhere to be seen. On the other hand, soldiers here and there were doing a lively Norwegian dance called *halling*—Nakadai and his comrades thought those soldiers were not only unpatriotic but dorks. Meanwhile, the medical tent was nearby with stretchers carrying bodies emptying out of it at a stunning rate. Nakadai had learned to look on coolly at such things, however, and decided to light a cigarette, dangle it from his lower lip like a flower stalk and conclude the card game. He didn't think the card game constituted a card game, however, because Yanagi changed the rules every 5 seconds.

Yanagi threw down her cards, Iga folded his arms pretending not to have an opinion and Kawaguchi asked if anyone wanted a drink. Nakadai put his hand up, so Kawaguchi nodded and went to the catering tent.

> *Drunk* and *intoxicated* are words that interest me. The *Old English past participle* "drink" suggests the same action carried out repeatedly. There is, too, the word used in reference to *habit*. E.g., "Nakadai's violent, drunken behaviour." Lastly, the word used in reference to cause and *effect*. E.g., "Nakadai is drunk—he is slurring his words!" The old Catholic understanding of *marital debt* was that, once married, each spouse owed to the other sexual intercourse. Thus, things are exchanged when I drink habitually.

Nakadai had regrettably taken to drinking heavily ever since the appearance of Father Conner in Saint Xavier's Cathedral.

There was a constant malevolent presence in Nakadai's mind, and Nakadai had decided to fight fire with firewater. Even the sight of Kawaguchi appearing out of the tent with beers in hand was enough to fill Nakadai with stirring hedonistic buzzes of pleasure. Kawaguchi returned to the miserable group of soldiers—in which Nakadai was the *most* miserable—and doled out the beers. Slowly, the pain of the world slipped away and everything was golden for a time. Kawaguchi had taken a sexual interest in Nakadai, but he had little to offer her since she was a woman. There had been a few rumours going around that Nakadai was gay, though these stories were about as frequent as the serpent's appearance in Haydn's *Creation*. In a confident attempt to see some skin, brought on by the alcohol he had ingested, Nakadai suggested they play a game of Flesh to pass the time. Kawaguchi and the others rolled their eyes because Nakadai seemed to enjoy this pastime a little *too* much when the men got involved. Nonetheless, they obliged him and nominated Iga to drop his trousers to below the buttock line.

He did this and waited for someone to slap his bum. The event occurred, after which he turned round because he had to guess whose hand was the culprit. He guessed it was Yanagi; he threw his hands up in admittance and replaced Iga's naked buttocks with *his* naked buttocks. Thus, the process was repeated again.

This time Nakadai was found to have slapped Yanagi's buttocks, so Nakadai duly had to drop his trousers and face away from the other players.

Unbeknownst to Nakadai, Kawaguchi had put her finger up to her lips. The others nodded as she picked up the plank of wood on two ammo boxes they had been sitting on.

Aiming to dole out an almighty wooden crack against Nakadai's cheeks, she misjudged the uneven earth and sent the plank hurtling instead against the back of Nakadai's head. The drunk Nakadai was knocked unconscious and fell onto the fertile soil, his sizeable *gluteus maximus* unmistakably naked in the jungle sunlight...

When Nakadai awoke in the field hospital, a piercing whine was addling his hearing and he immediately felt freedom. He felt the freedom to think his thoughts and freedom to laugh; it was as though the impact of Kawaguchi's wooden plank had pried Mutton's fingers away from Nakadai's soul. And Nakadai giggled to himself as the bandage on his head was skittishly unwrapped like a sun-softened sweet by a cute male nurse. Nakadai smiled insanely at the young man, hoping to make an impression, his confidence now boosted to what must have been maximum capacity; but the nurse's touch on the damaged private's head faltered, ceased altogether and Nakadai, once again, had been left alone with his thoughts.

"*Miminari ga suru.*" He beckoned the nurse back because his ears were ringing. He asked if his friend, Kawaguchi, was around.

Perplexed by the abnormal enthusiastic patient, the nurse hardened. "*O-kuyami moushiagemasu*," and sauntered methodically away—Why did he offer Nakadai his condolences?

(Kawaguchi, Yanagi and Iga had perished in the puerile conflict in the time between Nakadai's hospitalization and re-awakening.)

The piano works of Thelonious Monk were on Nakadai's mind when he received his honourable discharge from Japan's Self-Defence Force. There, unfortunately, was a mix-up with two medical forms where one soldier suffering *Capgras Delusion—the belief that everyone around him had been replaced with conniving doubles intent on destroying him*—was given a week of semi-instructed therapy at the nearest mainland hospital, after which he was given a free ticket to Tokyo, where, it has been said, this individual started a successful brokerage firm—whilst the mildly-concussed Nakadai was sent to a sanatorium versed in medieval cruelty in Yamanashi Prefecture. He was, effectively, taken there against his will and lived in abject emotional poverty for almost two years. Indeed, the Monkish compositions of *Off Minor* and *Blue Monk* seemed applicable to Nakadai's sudden existential deprivation.

> Have been taken to Yamanashi Sanatorium. They think I'm crazy. The sanatorium is made up of created beings which means there must be a *final cause*. Is this the work of the Great Word?

Nakadai's life in Yamanashi Sanitorium consisted of getting up early, jogging outside regardless of dangerous meteorological conditions, eating a monitored diet of cucumber slices and white rice, undergoing daily rigorous assessment by his psychiatrist, Otōmo, and ingesting a continuous stream of medication which not even Otōmo could fathom. There was, played over the speakers, a likewise continuous stream of *Five Tudor Portraits* by Vaughn Williams. Nakadai got to know the five musical portraits over those gruelling 23 months and could easily identify them as *Elinor Running*, *Pretty Bess*, *John Jayberd*, *Jane Scroop* and *Jolly Rutterkin*. Though they didn't play *Jolly Rutterkin* as much as they did the others.

One person who found this downright irritating was a Moldavian patient called Roxandra, who would play chess with Nakadai during the day and who, by some accounts, was one of the few people to have *sex* with Nakadai.

After these portions of the day, Nakadai would spend his time preparing for bed, going to bed and falling asleep in total silence—knowing he would do the same the following day.

His life had become mind-numbingly dull and purposefully structured and voiced these objections to Otōmo in his melon-shaped office situated in the sanitorium's gardens. Allegedly Otōmo scratched the underside of his chin, wrote down another medication with which Nakadai could be pumped, returned his melancholic gaze to Nakadai—the gaze of a man who had traded his firm belief in the curative values of face-to-face therapy for the ghastly empirical notion that the suffering would *always* suffer no matter their circumstances—and asked Nakadai if the original doctors (as opposed to the doubles) would agree with Nakadai.

> I would tell this man all the time: "I don't have whatever you think I have! This is an invalid marriage between us! And there are sufficient grounds for nullity! My name is Hiroshi Nakadai. I have a PhD in Theoretical & Applied Linguistics from the University of Twickley in England. That's a fact! You can check it, Otōmo!"

The psychiatrist never really acknowledged the words coming out of the ex-soldier's mouth, however, and would suffer Yamanashi Sanitorium's rarefied stratosphere for a long time after—the very same went for Nakadai, naturally.

The truth came to fruition finally in a flu-jab of luck, when the Liberal Party replaced the Nippon Progressives in government and ordered an investigation into the Tsushima War and the soldiers who had fought in it. Nakadai was suddenly like a choral singer in a production of Paganini's *Carnival of Venice* and wanted to jump and sing, "Mamma Mia!" amidst the various swirling costumes of Venetian lore. Despite this, Nakadai's relative sanity was proven to exist, and he was booted out of Yamanashi Sanitorium. He purchased a plane ticket back to Twickley and slept for an eternity when he got there...

7

IESU KIRISUTO—BURTON ABBEY —LUKA GRAF—ACADEMIA

My name is Nicola, and my back is starting to ache. When I started writing 50 minutes ago there was a lovely breeze coming through my window, drying the sweat on my forehead. If it's true that Wittgenstein made his own oxygen, I wish he'd come here and make some. I got rather sick of Mozart's *Hunt Quartet* and stuck on Kathleen Ferrier's performance in Britten's *Rape of Lucretia* instead—I do wish I had some cough syrup; then again, maybe it's the air and there is nothing there can do about it. That's a sobering thought, isn't it?

I'm getting distracted, however, and should make it clear to the reader that we've made it to the point in our narrative where things get soteriological and overtly holy.

Nakadai returned to England aged 29 with a mind to embark on a morally right-minded project that would last 12 years. The personal changes that would take place were so momentous that it becomes worthless attempting to describe them in a hastily assembled introductory paragraph that captures neither the gritty excitement nor the wretched injuries that Nakadai confronted—it is like reading an essay about the *Hammerklavier Sonata* and not actually hearing it, or like reading an essay about *Translations* and not actually *reading* it. Thus, we must turn to Nakadai's call to Iesu Kirisuto which saw him surprise his aunt, Ms. Chiba, with an idiosyncratic resolution that not even Ms. Chiba in her innumerable years of abundant gatherings and fortuitous episodes in and around her Asian Supermarket could have foreseen. Nakadai wanted to become a monk. "*Yare, nante koto da!*" cried Ms. Chiba; and what an ostensible disaster it must have appeared to have her nephew want to embrace the pensive life of a shaven monk—and a Catholic, Anglo-Saxon one at that? There would be no music that day in the Asian Supermarket—nothing but the ghost of Charles Mingus wandering from aisle to aisle with his shotgun, looking for the man who had so frightfully evicted him.

> There are *two* questions facing Catholicism in the modern world: 1.) How does one attain the same faith Saint Augustine had; 2.) What should the Catholic Church *do*? Ms. Chiba did not care about answering either question as she was inconsolable when I told her what *I* wanted to do. Since my parents had died, the job of shame-creation had fallen to Ms. Chiba. Her method involved telling me there wouldn't be a single Yokai who would forgive my formal conversion to Catholicism. She assured me the "wet woman" would come for me with her fake baby and vampiric tendencies. Did I take her at her word? Was she devout?

> I don't think she believed a damn thing she said. But she wanted to give me her pride when I told her I had no interest in getting married. (Japanese weddings have the very best dowries.) Apart from watching my parents dissolve into unhappiness, I did not tell her why I had no interest, that is, my homosexuality. I appreciated my family's traditions but there comes a time when one wants traditions of one's own. We all need our catechism.

In about a month, Nakadai became a monk and joined Burton Abbey in Huddersfield. The one-legged Abbot Cooney coolly welcomed Nakadai into the realm of the Benedictines warning the young man that it would not be as he had expected and that within the abbey it was a case of rules, rules, rules, worship, worship, worship. Abbot Cooney, who was not averse to the Soviet realism of Dmitri Kabalevsky's choral compositions, was something of a hypocrite, however; and the next 3 months were not unlike the experience Nakadai had had at Yamanashi Sanitorium. However, the hypocrisies in Burton Abbey seemed to be intensified by the surplus pastry flakes of Christianity.

Each day was segmented around mandatory services: one at midnight, one at 3:00 a.m. and one at 6:00 a.m. Terce, Sext and None before dinner. And Vespers at 6:00 p.m.

Throughout summer the monks would fast on Wednesday and Fridays and leave out their midday meal of fruit and fresh vegetables. Otherwise, each day consisted of cooking, portioning out food, washing up as well as cashing cheques and visiting the bank and doing an inordinate amount of reading and writing.

"We could barely talk to one another," Nakadai recalled. "Practically everything you said had to be either quiet or brief—but preferably both."

But the more we spoke of his time at Burton Abbey the more Nakadai struggled to speak. He knew we were like Parry's *Blest Pair of Sirens* and that the solemn music his words needed to convey would be better suited to one of his fictionalizations.

> I had just left the Yamanashi Sanitorium when the medication started to wear off. During my stay with Ms. Chiba, I became less and less addled by the drugs they'd been giving me and was dangerously close to death when I arrived at Burton Abbey.
>
> I was 29 years old when the annals of Benedictine monkdom outshone academia's and, within a month, I started thinking I had made a mistake. Then, quite by chance, I came into contact with a German monk called Luka Graf. His blonde hair and Habsburg jaw impressed me, and we became tentative lovers.
>
> The oil of saints flows from relics and burial grounds. That day, in the Abbey's garden, I was up to my neck in it.
>
> Luka was planting groundcover roses; his hands were covered in earth and he had his back to me. Behind him, I stepped across the olive-green grass with two bottles of water. I cleared my throat and he turned around, sweat rolling down his face.

He had just the right mixture of *innocence* and first-class *brains.*

"A frog is green by definition," I said.

"What the *fuck* did you just say?"

I smiled at his crude language. "A definition is a rule. Therefore, any object is characterized by a rule. And how do we break *free* of the rule? Well, we can *reject* the rule; we can reject *definition*; we can reject *projection* and finish with the present. We can speak *presently*. After all, Luka, to say a frog is purple is a one-off utterance."

Despite the *order of charity* that instructs us to love our neighbour, no matter their graveness, Luka's face was a corkscrew.

My flirtation had gone as smoothly as the founding of a theocracy. "Or something to that effect," I added as I stretched the bottle out.

He took the bait and the water bottle. He twisted off the cap, drank the forbidden clear liquid, and licked his lips.

I did the same then said, "Sprechen Sie Deutsch?"

"Ja. Machst du?"

"Nicht viel."

He giggled in disbelief when I told him I didn't speak much German. "Bist du zuversichtlich oder fließend?"

I said flatly, 'selbstsicher und fließend zu sein ist dasselbe."

With Luka, even the *four last things*—death, judgement, heaven and hell—would be bearable. They might even be *enjoyable*.

"Remarkable," Luka said.

"Ich habe dich laufen gesehen." It was true that I had seen him running.

Luka stopped laughing. *"Ja?"*

"Sie haben jetzt Problem emit dem Hügel, aber eines Tages warden Sie ihn hinauflaufen."

I'd seen him struggling up a certain hill. I told him he would make it, one day: "Ich weiß es..."

One has liberty with God's grace. One aspect of this liberty is the freedom of spontaneity. I do not *know* that I will be moved in different directions; only that I have the capacity to be guided. For the time being, I wanted *Luka* to guide me. I did not care *where*...

Here endeth the romantic tale. Whether asexual people just haven't found the right person yet, I have yet to understand. I must confess that my searching for a partner amongst my doctoral colleagues is not something to recommend. The quasi-esteemed, neurotic members of the academic body of doctoral candidates is just about the worst breeding ground for stable romantic partners you could imagine. Doubtless, reader, you recall my noisy neighbour from the postgraduate office? It pains me to say that, after some deliberation on my part, I confronted Stravinsky and asked him if he wanted to go for a coffee; assuming that he was single, of course.

"Yes, and *yes*," he replied.

"Seriously?" I couldn't believe it.

"I have to teach a seminar in an hour. But we could have coffee now."

"You don't need to prepare?"

"Well, no, because you're meant to prepare *in advance*." Stravinsky paused. "Which is what I do."

"Right," I said. "Do you want to go now, then?"

"Sure thang." And we walked to the Café Nero on campus, bought coffees and spoke for at least 50 minutes before he said, "You know, I just realized, I had my dates mixed up."

"What?"

"My seminar. That's tomorrow. I'm free all day."

"Right," I said, thinking I could go home and listen to Mozart's *Hunt Quartet* instead. "What do you want to do?"

"Are you horny?"

"I guess so," I replied, looking around me. "Where do you live?"

"Nearby, I'll take you..." Stravinsky, or whatever his name was, took me across campus to the car park. In the corner, on the very edge of existence, was a blue van. "Here we are!" he announced proudly.

"You live a *van*?" I disapproved.

"I'm self-funded, Nicola. We can't all live in castles as *you* do."

"I wouldn't call a one-bedroom flat a *castle*—"

The van wasn't *that* bad. I had seen doctoral students living in far worse conditions. Barrington Zapatero had lived in a tent, for example.

"What do you do for money?" I asked.

"Well, I'm what you'd call an *influencer*. I'm on Instagram if you want to follow me? I didn't want to freak you out during coffee. Bear with me." He took out his phone, took a photo of the two of us and said, "I'm just writing that I'm showing you my van—after all, the van is the motif."

We went in the van and got undressed. We had painful sex because I hadn't done it since Haydn's *Imperial Symphony* premiered. He then took a picture of the two of us and said, "I'm writing we just had sex."

"Say it was painful."

"Will do." He finished posting and turned to me: "I know we don't know each other that well...I just wanted to say...I'm not sure I'm the type of man you *need* right now..."

I softened. "Not the one I want, even?"

He shook his head. "No...I'm afraid not." The rain increase on the roof was louder than a badly-performed version of Gilbert & Sullivan's *Gondoliers.* "You see...I've been toying with the idea of heterosexuality, recently—"

"You don't like girls, then?"

"I thought I would try it out, you see, because at least then I'd know for sure. The scientific method—"

"The *crap* method—!" I quickly pulled on my sober clothes, opened the sliding door and stepped in the rain. "You don't *ever* get to complain about my musical habits, or—or anything! No more loud music in the office! You screwed this up; you *really* did!"

"You women are all the same!" replied Stravinsky.

"Yes, and the Elizabeth Sprague Coolidge Foundation *didn't* commission *Appalachian Spring*!"

"What the hell is *Appalachian Spring*?"

"And if you knew anything about music you wouldn't be asking *dumb* questions like that!" I stomped away from the van, across the car park and back to the postgraduate office.

Now, did this prove asexuality on my part? I wish it did because I had sex with Stravinsky, or whatever his name was, twice after that. You have to get what you can, in my experience; and my experience is pretty limited.

Anyway, it's true that Nakadai was homosexual and everyone seemed to know this. What they didn't think was that he would *ever* find a partner. That, however, is an autumn period we shall address presently—I must fashion a brand of truth from the shadows, the manifestly ill-lit series of events that followed as Nakadai cut much out from his soteriological ramblings, leaving me with a perplexing, silhouetted trademark of truth that not even Japan's Second Intelligence Department could capitalize upon. There are some details, however, that are worth getting down on paper:

Luka Graf's father was a man called Heinrich Freidrich Graf who was the head lawyer for the Reperio Society: an organisation that oversaw the operation of most universities in the United Kingdom—most notably the University of Twickley.

At some point, Luka informed Friedrich that he had been spending his evenings in gay clubs and the paterfamilias exploded with rage, removed him from his will and ordered him to attend Burton Abbey to alleviate his sins. It was a series of events that made Billie Holiday's fatal overdose look like a mere hiccup—her contribution to jazz and the careers of Count Basie and Artie Shaw notwithstanding.

Most probably those at Burton Abbey would have been aware of Luka's sexuality; on the other hand, Nakadai's sexuality was hardly a matter of interest, even if Abbot Cooney thought he was a bit queer in the near-prehistoric use of the word.

Put simply, Nakadai and Luka fell in love. They embarked upon a relationship that was fleshly, sensitive and loving. Though Nakadai seldom mentioned these words when describing their relationship in his letters to Ms. Chiba who, if she had known, would have suffered a cardiac arrest on the spot. Regardless, Nakadai and Luka went about courting as though they were an unaccompanied melody to which the texts of the Roman Catholic liturgy were sung; they were, in many ways, a binary *plainchant* and rhythmically free as they followed the prose rhythms of the psalms and prayers set by the terms of love. They hiked and cooked together in the kitchen; they studied the Bible with varied flushes of success and would cash the occasional cheque for Abbot Cooney. They began, in their limited capacity, to live together and shared a room in what proved to be a most fortuitous piece of accommodation planning on the part of Abbot Cooney's rooming committee.

As with all performances of *St. Paul's Suite*, however, there came a time when the excited strings gave way to the solitary fiddle—its cloistered nature represented the downward spiralling of any half-baked, romantic relationship. Nakadai and Luka would argue about things neither man could define in rational terms. They traded books and would talk extensively about Nakadai's beloved Inspector Miller novels; except these were also the favoured texts of Abbott Cooney, which doubtless led Luka to believe that Cooney was sleeping with Nakadai and not *him*. He made accusations that Nakadai was rogering the Abbott and stealing money from the abbey's accounts. Both were rumours cooked up by Luka, regrettably. This was the beginning of that great betrayal in which Nakadai was caught not only in the crossfire but also, ostensibly, holding a dangerous loaded weapon himself. There was subsequent unmitigated upheaval at the abbey with Nakadai being accused by Luka of ratting him out to the other monks, which he would never have done as he loved Luka with a fiery passion: a char-grilled passion as far as Nakadai was concerned, and would never have committed anything that might have injured his beloved Luka. This was an amorous entanglement, unquestionably, which sparked intimacy and precise playing of the kind demonstrated by *Harriet Cohen*; that talented British pianist to whom Vaughn Williams dedicated so many compositions of his own. When I pressed Nakadai for details, however, he got stroppy and foul-mouthed:

> There's a tendency in the Catholic Church to think about the future in *happy* terms. How can I talk about happiness when there are secrets to be kept? What reasons are there for keeping secrets? I want to look normal, and contrary to the opinions of my department, I succeed where others fail. I want to protect people, also. You destroy a thing by *depriving* it. You destroy information by *not* speaking about it. Luka twisted our relationship and destroyed it. He had outward blessings and inward horrors. However, he was a human being and does

> *not* deserve to be treated unfairly by posterity—and posterity is *vulgar* in any case. When you don't speak about something you destroy it. There is, too, the divine reason for secrets. There is something to be said about *quietism*: that in order to be perfect one must be totally passive. I can for example reserve judgement. I struggle with that and even now am struggling to prevent my judging *you*, Nicola. In any case that's the end of the matter...

The end of the matter would not be the verbal insensitive spurning of a postgraduate who had asked too many questions, but the death of a single monk.

After an argument where Luka had been acrimonious and fuming and Nakadai foppish and insensitive, Luka stormed out to Abbott Cooney's Edsel Villager Replica, produced the keys from his pocket (as he had stolen them the previous day), opened the door and stepped inside. He keyed the ignition and sped off down curly sylvan roads and jammed his foot on the accelerator. He quickly swerved to avoid another car when it peered out of a driveway, skidded on the road that was wet with the silk of the morning and crashed disastrously into an oak tree. Luka then stumbled out of the car and stared up at the sky. "No," he shouted, "not yet!" But according to a local farmer, Luka nodded and then fell over into a thesaurus of leaves. One might say that Weber's *Invitation to the Dance* had been declined, and Luka succumbed to his head injuries and passed away.

Things were grave and panic ensued. Nakadai had neither partner nor excuses and would soon be without his vocation.

He thought solemnly of Handel's *Julius Caesar* and decided to call upon the only person who could help. This was neither Handel nor Shakespeare, for both were quite dead, but Professor Mutton—and this substantially less talented man picked up the phone and audibly grinned with glee at the 39-year-old's gruesome and ill-fated predicament:

> He made me beg. The Egyptian cross, with its looped, perpendicular bar bears the ancient meaning of life. Thus, when I begged Professor Mutton to find me a job, I knew for me that life would thenceforth hold that ancient, distant position. I accepted that another chapter of my life was ending when I left Huddersfield for the last time. Then, upon entering Twickley, I remembered that since there was no question about the eternal duration of heaven, we had to assume the same for hell. I accept the options were scarce at that time, but I should never have chosen hell...

8

FULTON ROAD—LECTURESHIP—EIKO EGAMI—BASHFUL LANE—DAXX FREUDENBERGER

The consequences of Nakadai's overdue return to academia were significant and bottled any reasonable chance Nakadai had of leading a spiritual life. The extemporary apartment that Nakadai would inhabit for the next year was on Fulton Road and had a small ochre-coloured kitchenette with sublimely grouted tiles and a positively polar bathroom in which a toilet with a rubbery plastic seat was rattled by the precipitous chilly winds outside. The living room was uninhabitable as far as Nakadai was concerned—for directly beneath his deaf neighbour's television set blasted immature hubbubs from lunchtime to midnight. This would have been fine had there been, blasting from the television set Haydn's *Clock Symphony*, Beethoven's *Grosse Fuge* or Handel's *Hallejuah*. Nakadai, by his admission, would have been happy with *Sly & The Family Stone*—but instead, he was treated to Lil Wayne, Rebecca Black, Iggy Azalea and retired albums of *Kidz Bop*; and dear reader, I task you to wonder: what kind of old woman *was* this?

Regardless, the bedroom featured a faux-birch wardrobe that boasted neither shelves nor doors while next door there was a many-locked and bulky front door which led down a snail-shellish coil of stairs. At the base of the staircase were his neighbour's smelly bin bags which mutilated the dank, single-bulbed hallway with the odours of decaying chicken carcasses and broccoli stalks.

A significant regression from the cosy Benedictine double-dormitories and their erstwhile promises of raunchy carnal ecstasy, without a doubt—but Nakadai had consented to perform the complex, philosophical music of Toshiro Mayuzumi, in a manner of speaking, and was prepared to pay the price for his bondaged freedom with loyalty. Professor Mutton made Nakadai an Assistant Lecturer in Neo-Linguistics which meant that Nakadai would teach within an established programme of study, develop teaching methods and approaches, supervise the work of both undergraduate and postgraduate students, connect whenever possible with other research institutions (universities) and actively participate as a member of a teaching team. Nakadai shuddered at this prospect—for, very few academics enjoy teaching—but consented to teach the comprehensive undergraduate NL1311 course. In the meantime, Professor Mutton met with Nakadai privately to discuss work on the Word Machine.

> He may have sounded gleeful on the phone, but in person, his body was decaying. He had reached a point of discouragement with *his* situation. Small, grey

pustules ran up and down his hands, and his frame reeked of death. We were slaves to the Great Word and he was suffering the consequences as I was reaping the benefits. Truth be told I did not know his age—his *real* age. He had reached the end, regardless, and I was his last *act of hope*. He had worked tirelessly on the Word Machine and had produced nothing. His designs and subsequent equations were always wrong and had produced some terrifying inventions. The Grammar Engine had turned an unsuspecting undergraduate into an unknown verb; the Lexicon Loosener had erased the word *chicken* from everyone's minds; the Text Motor had paralysed Professor Mutton's knowledge of *nouns* and he, in the time before reclaiming this knowledge, spent a long time trying to order *something* from Café Nero. He had put these disasters behind him when his body had started giving up. Now I had re-entered the picture, and he was adamant I would succeed where he (and others) had failed.

"You seem to think the bridge won't fall down," said Mutton. "It's not a question of physics, Nakadai, your time is running out. No good will come of your fiddling with contradictions; just a load of puzzles, that's all: I want something concrete!"

Indeed, God's folio of coincidence and consequence had worked in Professor Mutton's favour so far. Meanwhile Mutton laughed inwardly despite his intimate pains:

> "If you *don't* help me, I will let the Great Word penalize you. You want to dedicate your brain to logic, formalism and intuitionism, but in my master's presence, you'll find lifting a finger a miserable experience. You're in my employment. That's something beyond empirical science, I would like you to remember it. The university...is a *mask*: it doesn't care about your work, but our master, the Great Word, unremittingly *does*...and you shall manufacture its entrance!"
>
> I agreed and soon found myself drawing no distinction between matter and spirit (*Hylozoism*), such was my concentration from the offset. I had a most regrettable past; I knew Professor Mutton could give me a most regrettable future—I was aged 39. I was still alive, somehow. I had never reached beyond myself so I must have had *humility*. Except I *was* ignorant of God's gifts, and in their place, I made Professor Mutton a relic and worshipped him by exercising my amazing brain. Was he aware I would pit my brain *against* him? If so, what preparations could he make? We were *both* slaves...

How gruelling it was, though, to approach any kind of favourable outcome in the Department of English Language & Linguistics.

Nakadai may very well have made a Faustian pact with the servant of an intergalactic being known as the Great Word, but this seemed nothing to his trouble adapting to the realm of academia. One fellow academic overseas, Dr. Eiko Egami, had been feeling similarly about her professional predicament. She lectured in Creative Writing at the Tokyo Media School and, against the advice of her department, began authoring a series of anti-academic stories and novels. Nakadai was fascinated by her cynicism and read everything he could get his hands on. Determined to understand his situation, he authored the following essay on *Eiko Egami*—a piece of writing I believe to be the equivalent of Mozart's *Musical Joke*, a satire of the work of provincial composers with atonal chords and coarse progressions *par excellence*.

> I believe it was Eiko Egami who once said, "As for those who want to talk about metaphysics and language, I hope they all die in a violent car crash, one of those where you can barely recognise the car afterwards." I was depressed when I heard she had committed suicide. Her brain was exemplary in its *wrongness*. I have tried to explain this to many people and, weather prevailing, no one has *ever* agreed with me. I thought for some time about this. Egami's brutal nature; her bloodlust for logic was a wedge that drove her from her colleagues. Perhaps she never thought of them as colleagues but as vermin in the Tokyo Media School. And after a mediocre career as a lecturer in Creative Writing, she jumped *off* the Tokyo Media School, landing on the Vice Chancellor's car. It was *quite* the sight: the body mangled; the apparent bones frilled; the expression on her face as though she

had seen God. I believe that God is omnipotent. The actions God takes are never self-contradictory. God is infinite in *being* as well as *power*. Thus, nothing self-contradictory is beyond God's power. The case of Eiko Egami, then, points towards her being a direct contradiction to God. This is not the most popular view I have taken on a subject. I believe she was from the dark side. She had come to destroy us and, when God saw her power, was destroyed herself.

Everyone has a set of beliefs. And when people asked Egami she identified most strongly with Quentin Mugg and Sarah-Jane Blutarch (*Muggism* and *Blutarchanism*, respectively).

Quentin Mugg was a Nigerian critical theorist and William Blake scholar who espoused the idea that each text had to be examined in a vacuum. Not a theoretical vacuum but an *actual* vacuum that he had built as an extension to his rather nice apartment near Bowen University in Iwo. Meanwhile, Sarah-Jane Blutarch was a mathematician and criminally underrated bassoon player (according to Nicola Hillam-Joiner) who was famous for *Blutarch's Grand Reciprocation*. Her *Reciprocation* reversed Zermelo-Fraenkel Set Theory and reinstated paradoxes into mathematics. Overnight, two million PhDs became meaningless, most mathematics became *meaningless* and the number of people applying for PhDs in Literature went through the roof. Blutarch approached the resurrection of paradoxes with an ethical bent and gave long, indulgent speeches about it at commencement ceremonies. However, Sarah-Jane Blutarch was a homophobe and retired from public life when it was discovered that Ernst Zermelo and Abraham Fraenkel had been lovers.

Eiko Egami was influenced by a guy with a vacuum and a homophobe. But it would be wrong to say this wasn't worth my consideration. We must never forget the academic world in which she lived because her environment made her *believe* in a guy with a vacuum and a homophobe.

I have known *many* academics. They are self-aware, improvisational and unimaginative. They follow rules in much the same way. They usually have an allegiance to Marxism, Socialism, Conservatism, Muggism, Blutarchanism, or *what-happened-after-*Modernism. They are *brave* people; they attend departmental meetings; they eat sticks and things from Tupperware; they have no money and speak constantly of people in history who *also* had no money. But Eiko Egami did none of these things. She was *not* brave; she was penalized for *not* attending departmental meetings; she would eat breakfast, lunch and dinner in expensive restaurants; her wealth came from trading cryptocurrency on the weekends, and she hated everyone who had *ever* lived.

I am not surprised, with her *modus operandi*, that she went insane. But what about her colleagues? The ones that, unlike her, outlived and out-performed

Egami? There was the red-haired Yori Aoki, who had published 20 monographs on *Continental Nipple*; Daichi Murakami, who specialized in literature written in the *Abun* language—which, given only 3,000 people speak *Abun*, make those tribes in Papa New Guinea the most literarily prolific population in the world; Tomi Ōta, who had proven using undiscovered sources that Billie Eilish *was*, in fact, a CIA agent in the mould of *Red Sparrow*; Sachiko Kaneko, who took the Berkeley-inspired line that the films of Quentin Tarantino did *not* exist when you turned away from them; and Teru Matsuda, who had edited a collection of essays on the logical impossibility of frankness in the novels of David Foster Wallace. Egami was unimpressed, however, because she lived for disruption. Aware she was living in a world dictated by zero-sum games she intended to break with logical tradition and be *herself*. For, if one reduces every single human interaction to a *zero-sum* game, a game where there can only be *one* winner, the objective is to win; not to withhold and withstand empirical science or logic. Egami understood that decision-making in a zero-sum game was totally rational; the rationality being to win even at the cost of reality. Thus, the game perpetuates itself through its players' complex desires now reduced to simple, cold survival. Egami destroyed this when she became herself. The paranoid network of attack that *is* the capitalist world of zero-sum games was now without a player. Would there be more like her? If so, the whole system would cease to function with people becoming themselves all over. The world would end; a positive apocalypse. I cannot play a game of chess by myself, and Egami understood this implicitly. Her powers went beyond criticism and pierced souls. But she did not die in a car crash...

In May Professor Mutton allowed Nakadai to move from his extemporary apartment on Fulton Road to an even less residential—but more functional and quieter apartment on Bashful Lane. Nakadai would live here for the rest of his life. The shimmering apartment was half-furnished with orangey carpets pinpointing the centre of each room. There was the substantially larger kitchen complete with an electric oven, large extractor fan and 'shrubbish, tree-lined view from the window over the modest marble sink, and the master bedroom Nakadai filled with a used mattress purchased sneakily in the half-price district of Clourn. Nakadai found, as all who listen to the ballet works of *Ferroud* find, delightful concentration in a tiny study room where Nakadai erected his picnic table—purchased, similarly, from Homebase. This he covered with multicoloured allotments of books.

Lastly, there was the sober panelled bathroom with a shaky-sided bathtub adjacent to a wooden-seated toilet whose flush mechanism consisted of a long, knobbed string that dangled from the ceiling like a note Cleo Laine might have sung during her time with *John Dankworth's Orchestra.*

Nakadai was on the ground floor. He received the post and attended on occasion the shambolic yellowish blob that was the front garden. He never heard a peep from the elderly female living upstairs. Her television murmured in temporary bashful slots which Nakadai reasoned was the rationale for delicately deciding to live on Bashful Lane. There was music murmured only occasionally, and for the most part, it was Byzantine music that led Nakadai to believe she was probably Armenian or Greek—but her story is private, and belongs to her alone.

The move to Bashful Lane—in that manner so often described by Frederick Douglass—made everything smooth and events go smoothly. By way of comparison, the *double-flat* sign exists to reduce a note's pitch by a whole tone. If this lowering of Nakadai's tone was smooth, then, it was also anything but easy considering the inauspicious supernatural bondage that Nakadai had willingly subscribed to at the behest of the scheming Professor Mutton.

> I moved to Bashful Lane and felt like a member of the Catholic resistance in Japan during the 17th Century. There were many children in the resistance. I felt, however, like a Catholic writer forced to produce a *temple-affiliation certificate* on a sunny day. These feelings were amplified when I met Daxx Freudenberger, who lived a few doors down. He was studying medicine at the university, pasty-faced with sedimentary waves of blonde hair. He looked *exactly* like Luka Graf, and there was something simple about him: he had the *right* mixture of innocence and first-class brains, I thought.
>
> That morning, when I introduced myself, I had imagined taking him to *mandatum* and washing his

feet during the Liturgy of Holy Thursday. I longed to show Daxx that *novum mandatum*—to love as God had loved *us*.

I explained I worked at the university. I welcomed the sallow postgraduate into my living room and admired his gangling arms and trainers which were the same shade of green *mine* were.

We talked for a long time about *isolation*. "When Christianity was outlawed in Japan," I said, "The worshippers went underground. Figures of the Virgin Mary were whittled and dressed to resemble the Buddha. Prayers were adapted, linguistically, to resemble Buddhist chants; it was all an effort to *conceal...*"

He was unimpressed when I told him this. "Do you like chess?" I asked.

"Of course. Here, let me help you—"

"What are you doing?"

"I'm was just gonna walk you over to the board."

"Why?"

"You're blind, aren't you?"

"No, I am *not* blind!" I complained. "What on *earth* gave you that impression?"

"The way you were looking at me. Never mind, it's no problem."

"Indeed," I commented as I sat in the nearest beach chair. "Shall we begin?"

He sat down whereupon he slapped his thigh. "*Dulce periculum*!"

"Sweet danger, yes." I picked our queens up and fiddled behind me. "Which hand?"

"Hold up there, cowböy, I've got to explain the rules. Basically, a chess board has 64 divisions or squares and they alternate between black and white. Every square receives an identification which is used in *chess notation*, of which there are several kinds. There is *descriptive algebraic* and *numeric* notation. You're a newbie so I'll start easy: *numeric* notation is where each subdivision has a two-digit designation. So, if your Rook moves from square 81 to square 84 the notation for that would be 8184. *Sehr einfach*. You can trust me, too, because I study neuroscience, which, I have to tell you is a real pain the *unterseite*—"

I commandeered the monologue. "Daxx, I don't know the rules—"

"There you go then—"

"But I *am* aware of them, shall we say. I'd rather not bring the problem of certainty into our little match. Now, choose a hand."

He pointed at my right hand. It was the white queen, so it was his move.

"Why?" he said.

"Because you're white."

"You people in the Humanities are *all* the same—"

"Make the first move! I need something to react to!"

He pouted. "I'll move—but you won't *like* it."

He moved his pawn 4244. I moved my Knight 7866, and the game lasted for 5 minutes.

"Nobody knows how the Virgin Mary died, you know? What I do know is...*checkmate*."

"Nein."

"Ja."

He was offended. "You speak *German*?"

"Nicht viel."

"Liar." He slapped his thigh once more. "I'll be *verflucht*." He paused again. "You said you needed something to react to. Why say *that*, and not something else?"

"I have asked that question my whole life. Why say one thing, and not something else?" I harumphed. "How absurd."

"And the game?"

"To win. Do you hear that?" I spoke to the Great Word in the sky. "I'm going to win." I sat back in my beach chair and sighed. "The options and architectures in chess are so manifold and contingent upon so many different things that even to *behave* as though you *understand* chess must rank among the very worst mental illnesses. The most I can do when you make a move is to *react*; and to bear in mind, at all times, that I don't *know* how to play chess—especially when there is nothing to know about chess that can't be taught in 5 minutes, which is how long our little match lasted."

Daxx touched his belly. *"Ich werde krank."*

"If you're going to be sick, then do it outside. The worms will love it."

> Leaving him to stew in his *samsara*, I relinquished my carnal desires and showed him out. I went back inside, quickly, and wept...

Nakadai's sex life was practically non-existent around this time. I hasten to add such details because early on in our discussions it became clear to me that his restrained libido and his sense of intellectual righteousness were joined at the groin. In other words, there was a kind of carnal ecstasy experienced and on display to others when Nakadai engaged in conversation. Especially a conversation in which he found himself—as he always did—to be staggering up a mountain of veracious observations, whilst his compatriots behind him struggled even to see the mountain. The jousting seen in an intellectual discussion can often be political. Thus, Nakadai must have been the most *politically incorrect* of opponents; his argumentation adorning the tone of anti-Papist *liliburlero* songs heard in Ireland shortly after General Talbot was appointed to govern the country in 1687. Despite his tears after Daxx Freudenberger's departure, moments like these were necessarily welcomed by the lonely and sex-less Nakadai. But they were seldom sustained for any great deal of time as the immense chilling afterthought each day returned to him that he was in the worst kind of intellectual bondage.

His drinking escalated briefly when, despite the minor concussion sustained from the plank during his military duty, the voices in his head returned. The concussion might have shaken Professor Mutton's psychological exertions on Nakadai; the spiritual life at Burton Abbey might have prevented such evil authorities from thriving in the aging monk's skull; but Nakadai's return to Mutton's diabolical abstract embrace confirmed how the Great Word's organs of speech, buried deep within his mind, were gradually gaining power and would possibly shatter Nakadai's senses. He *knew* that he was on the cusp of academic brilliance with his first book *Translations* nearing its final draft; the linguistic equivalent of Vivaldi's lasting development of the *three-movement concerto* which would later be imitated by Bach and others. Put simply, nothing could stand in the way of this; Nakadai understood his life *depended* upon it. He concluded that he needed a second pair of hands. The most viable option, unfortunately, was nowhere to be seen at the University of Twickley. Thus, Nakadai opted to head-hunt the individual himself, and this shall be the topic of the subsequent chapter in our narrative.

9

GORO SAITO'S CAREER—DEVIL DRUG—DANIELLE FURLOUGH—DIVORCE

Dr. Saito as his sixth formers had called him led a curious career after receiving his PhD in Theoretical & Applied Linguistics—much like Jascha Horenstein giving up conducting after he took up Swiss citizenship, or Franco Alfano deciding to *not* write 20 operas. His curious career is compounded by his reluctance to answer any questions about Nakadai who served periodically as a friend, colleague and editor. (To my knowledge Saito lives in Newcastle; he was last seen volunteering at the Red Cross and singing in their yuletide choir.) The truth is that whereas Nakadai was entirely open, unblushing but impenetrable, Saito was in all respects tight-lipped, deliberate but undemanding when it came to negotiating his personality. He was my secondary tutor, after all, and would offer unhelpful, but not unfriendly, advice when he wasn't gossiping about me in the departmental corridor. For some reason, he seemed terrifically happy to see me when he was getting *off* the bus and I was getting on it. In the way *Martha*

Argerich had only secured her reputation as one of the finest pianists of her generation when she won the Warsaw Chopin Competition, I desperately wished that Goro Saito would be recognized for his work, and thus lift him out of his impenetrable aloofness.

Early on Nakadai decreed that his friend and colleague Goro Saito was a bog-standard academic and that his appeal was the very bog-standardness that prevented him from having a pronounced public persona of his very own. Thus, I shall relay only what Nakadai told me of his friend, which does not aggravate our narrative but merely incarcerate it in the chronic lingual world of Nakadai—which is no vexation comparable to Haubenstock-Ramati's collaborating with Samuel Beckett on his theatre show *Credentials*. For, as you shall see, dear reader, enclosed in Saito's bog-standardness was an imperative sensory faculty for what was good and evil in the world. I will not dwell on his relentless pursuits in these matters; but merely focus on one conversation in which his imperative sensory faculty reared its positive head, then work forward from there to where we are *temporally* in our narrative. Nakadai, who was a biographically-gifted writer in his own right, apparently *enjoyed* writing about Saito. His fictional renderings of the colleague in question are, perhaps, more enjoyable to read than Goro would be to encounter. With that in mind, I have copied out the following tale.

> It was hot that February. The pavements were dry around campus, and so was the square. My lanyard did not work that day. I was forced to work in the library;

the same went for Goro, and his friend, Alia, who talked too much and studied physics (in that order).

There was no air-conditioning in the library. We were forced to go outside and breathe occasionally. Goro would remove his socks and dry them on his shoulders. Alia would smoke a yellow cigarette. I would watch them, breathing heavily, the occasional pigeon grabbing my attention.

"I tell you guys," Alia said, "I'm about to crack. The first day I was here, I remember, this lady asked me if I had a desk. I told her I didn't, and she gasped. She couldn't believe it. Then she explained she was the person whose *job* it was to get PhD students desks. And I couldn't believe *that*. I tell you guys, I'm gonna do something. I'm gonna go crazy."

"It's too late for that," Goro said.

"You're right, man. Do you know what I do on the weekends? In the library? I bring one of my books from home, I go to the return scanner and pretend to return my book. Then I find a librarian and say, 'This won't let me return it.' They'll look it up and say, 'We don't have that book.' And I'll say that I don't want to besmirch the name of this library. And they ought to know what books they have because I *definitely* got this book from the library and I won't leave until it's been returned according to procedure. These librarians lose their minds, they get their bosses and look all over the place. Then I just slip out the way I came. It drives them *nuts*."

"That's *mean*," I said.

"The other day I managed to get *into* my office. I see this huge rock stuck in my shoe; I have to use pliers to get it out. I chuck it out the window; it lands next to some freshers. They look up and say, 'What do you think you're doing? You could hurt someone!' And I just lean out and shout, 'Get real motherfuckas! Living like a doctor!'"

"I wonder," I said, "what God would think about me if he were here."

Alia blew out smoke. "You can't avoid God. He or she is everywhere."

"Maybe. What if there was a drug that stopped you from committing sins?"

"Mate, he's a *proper* Catholic." Alia jabbed Goro's be-socked shoulder. "Run a mile."

"He doesn't *bite*, Alia."

"I'm sure he's kinky." The physics doctorate coughed. "Alright, Nakadai. You want a drug like Mormons want magic underwear."

"It's Latter-Day Saints who wear *temple garments*. And you haven't even brought up the *real* problem."

"What's that? Your mother?"

"*No*," I said gently. "If evil is contingent upon our actions, it makes little sense for a single action like taking a pill to suddenly end all contact with evil things."

"Where's Max Planck when you need him?" Alia whistled at some men going to play hockey. "Are you seeing anyone, Nakadai?"

I blushed.

"I wish I was." Her thick eyebrows raised. "Goro, what's that man in your department? The one with the limp."

"The limp?"

"Yea, dreadlocks."

"Omar Braddock?"

"Yea, that's him. I saw his name on a poster. I'd suck his dick. I'd suck it and suck it, Nakadai, I'd suck it till there was nothing left. I went drinking with some undergraduates the other night. One of them sidled up to me and said, "If I were a lecturer, I'd just fuck as many students as possible." Now *that* is a good philosophy."

"No, it's not," I said. "It's unprofessional and hurts people."

There were early Jewish Christians who still followed Mosaic laws: they practiced circumcision and dietary laws. Some were devout Christians and others were heretical Gnostics—whenever I spoke to Alia the dichotomy had a similar volatility.

Alia laughed. "Now you have *got* to be on some drugs."

"Why do I need medication when I have *you*?"

"Shots have been fired!" Goro checked up on his socks. "Maybe you *do* need that Devil Drug!"

I grew nervous. The *justification* of theology is a double-edged blade. On the one hand my growing into a *state of grace* is sufficient justification, but so too are my sins being removed.

I said, "Life is *so* delicate."

Alia stamped out her cigarette. "Yep."

"I think about children making amends with their parents. When they don't want to. I think *that* is evil."

Goro shrugged. "But supposing they *took* your Devil Drug; it wouldn't guarantee their making amends ever; whether they liked it or not."

"Why, then, do we want to *avoid* evil? You can't avoid evil any more than you can *good*. And people are more frightened of doing good than evil."

"Not everyone is *you*, Nakadai," said Alia. "If you're down I could *give* you something."

"Your druggy sideline may *haunt* you," Goro proffered, "but this is *not* the place for a confession."

The voluntary self-accusation of one's sins. "You can't do that anyway."

"Yes, I *can*, Nakadai." Alia's hair stood on end. "I know for a fact secular people got to confession. It's the power of physics."

"Explain."

"Father Conner had one who couldn't stop crying: a prison guard on death row in Cornwall. They've had capital punishment down there ever since they went independent. This guy called Oscar Heligan shoots a waiter and takes the restaurant hostage. The police show up and negotiate a surrender. Oscar comes out and shoots the negotiating officer. He escapes the police and goes to Falmouth to see his mother's grave. And he puts the gun to his head and pulls the trigger."

"Jesus," I said.

"It gets worse. The gunshot *didn't* kill him. The police find him and take him to the hospital. He recovers but it's like he had a lobotomy. He has basic motor functions and can talk. He certainly can *eat*. But he's not the man who committed those murders. The police and families don't care; he's put on trial and gets two counts of first-degree murder. He gets sentenced to death. The prison guard I mentioned before; she was the guard who brought Oscar Heligan his last meal."

I had tears in my eyes. "What was it?"

Her brow furrowed and she said, "He had black coffee and a sausage roll with coleslaw. He ate the roll and drank the coffee, and when they said it was time to leave, he said he'd finished the coleslaw later. The prison guard couldn't believe it: he couldn't comprehend his surroundings. But they took him to the special room and executed him with lethal injection. And that was that."

"And the prison guard was confessing all this?"

"She did. She doesn't believe in God. How could you after *that*?"

Goro put his socks back on. "I'm going back inside."

I had voices in my head. It was easy to believe in God. For a long time, I thought the Great Word was God but that was impossible. No God would hatch a plan involving me. That was *far* too risky...

With the genesis of their friendship out of the way, I must briefly describe how Saito subsequently received his PhD in Theoretical & Applied Linguistics with only minor revisions. He went on a pub crawl with Alia and was ejected from *The Loopy Boot* when he remarked to the landlady's face that she had "an unusually powerful pair of booty-cheeks". Saito and Alia were later arrested for loitering outside the police station as they were trying to figure out what Delius's *Mass of Life* was all about; there was no doubting, for example, that the words taken from *Thus Spake Zarathustra* were indeed beautiful, if somewhat fruity, but this left the arresting police officer with even *less* to say when he brought them inside to the rather embarrassing befuddlement of the officer-on-duty. The following morning Saito tried to put his relationship with Alia in the past and move on to greener pastures. Nakadai understands that he got lost for a bit, in the existential sense, and worked briefly at the Twickley Homebase where he attained the rank of G4.

> I have found that many academics have a sense of *ethical duty*—they try to do good no matter how the legal establishment reacts to their actions. It would take a long time for me to remind Goro of *his* ethical duty. There is something odd about an academic person working at Homebase. When the question of money arises, I can see the practical reason but disagree on an ethical one. My quarrel is not with Goro but with contemporary culture. They provide the linens of higher education in England except they do not *care* about bioscience, literature or

chemistry—unless it benefits the checks and balances of capitalism, of course.

Saito found a job teaching English at Cheltenham College after leaving Homebase. He packed his things, moved out of his apartment in Twickley and appeared in Cheltenham out of thin air. He found an apartment and a girlfriend and began a scholastic life at the college. He affected these changes with the baritonic control of John Shirley-Quirk as well as the myriad disgruntlement I experienced when I realized how much of John Sheppard's music was missing from our English archives of pre-Reformation music.

Discounting Sheppard's lost choral masterpiece, for example, throughout these 18 years Saito lost contact with Nakadai who, in the meantime was called to military service and mistakenly sent to a ludicrous medieval sanitorium. He had then become a monk for a considerable time only for that monkish life to be terminated by the death of a loved one; forcing him to take a job at the University of Twickley.

Saito, meanwhile, had risen through the ranks of the Cheltenham College English Department and married an English woman called Betty Fielding-Malice—who, incidentally, was not the same woman he dated when first arriving in Cheltenham. Briefly, Betty was a talented cello player who toured both nationally and internationally; her claim to fame was her arranging for cello every number written by Lionel Hampton, the jazz band leader who introduced the *vibraphone* to popular music. Combined with Goro Saito's efforts to finish writing his book, *The Open Verb*, which sought to interpret previous interpretations of the work-language *Tongutire*, the marriage lasted 5 years and both went through a nasty divorce because, as it turned out, their respective lawyers had once been married themselves and took the case as an opportunity to settle some old debts. That Michaelmas Term saw Saito become Head of English at Cheltenham College, however, and Saito signed the publishing contract for *The Open Verb* and collapsed in his new office.

It was around that time that Nakadai read voraciously *The Open Verb* and deemed Saito to be a linguistic *virtuoso*. Putting to one side the length of time which had passed, he decided to head-hunt the gangly Goro in his hour of need and surreptitiously attained the man's phone number from an undisclosed source. The negotiations for Saito's joining the Department of English Language & Linguistics at the University of Twickley had little to do with linguistics; these negotiations would prove to be the *Gaspard de la Nuit* in Ravel's otherwise rock-solid oeuvre. Saito, notwithstanding his totemic grasp of good and evil, had fallen by the wayside personally, since what had led to his divorce in the first place—a series of insolent selfish activities which provided ammunition to the most bloodthirsty colleagues—was a woman called Danielle Furlough who had slept with Saito several times during his marriage to Betty Fielding-Malice. Furlough, like Fielding-Malice, was a musician and made her living translating the baroque musicology of Austrian-British organist *Susi Jeans*. Naturally, Fielding-Malice and Furlough became great friends when the affair and marriage were over; and they would leave Saito to consider the consequences of his actions. And so, the negotiations conducted between Nakadai and Saito fell (or arose) entirely to prolonged discussions of his affair, one of which Nakadai committed again to a memoirish fictionalization.

Goro was a tall-sounding man. His words were elongated, somehow, sounding like rubber bands snapping to and fro. I was a *benefice* that day: a juridical entity who had received a blessing from an ecclesiastical authority—the University of Twickley.

"There *really* is too much to talk about," I said into the phone. "What do you know about the Harris Treaty?"

Goro coughed. "Educate me."

"The Harris Treaty of 1858 allowed foreigners to live in Japan. For the first time, people flocked to our country. Even clergymen were allowed to come—though they couldn't convert anyone. That was against the law. I say this because I feel to be in a similar position with *you*, Goro. I'm trying to see if you've changed but I don't want to *convert* you in any way. I wonder—who told you about the sky?"

"The sky? That's the gay club you told me about, isn't it?"

"I deny everything." I scribbled the name down. "I mean the word-thing in general."

"I probably learned about *the sky* at nursery?"

"When you were a tiny squid?" I squeezed the bridge of my nose. "Sorry, I didn't mean—"

"What did you call me? *Tiny squid?*"

"Yes, never mind; a slip of the tongue. But the only reason," I continued, "you and I can talk about this thing called *the sky* is because someone mentioned it and then *pointed up*. A connection between *uttered-word* and *thing-seen*?"

When the Great Word had come, all this would end. The multiple labels, names and designations would become one perfect word. The *vault of heaven* and the *blue yonder* would no longer be needed. Nor would the *welkin*, the *ether* or the *azure*. We would all succumb to singularity.

"I suppose so," said Goro.

"This whole thing where we name something and point towards it instigates a *deeper* question." That is the depth of philosophy; *religious indifference* becomes water in a skillet. "The problem is whether we can question something that isn't tangible—like God."

"Which is a name."

"There are infinite names, forms and shapes. That *is* the essence of God."

"Hold up." I could hear Goro thinking. It was raining where he was. "When you question the existence of something you don't take issue with its *matter*, but with its *label*."

"Thus, an object, in itself, is never investigated." I crossed my legs. "Maybe all we *have* is theological truth."

"Oh no." I could hear Goro lean over the phone. "You're not *religious*, are you?"

"You knew I was Catholic, didn't you? I had aspirations at university but when I got back from Japan, I was made a Catholic proper. I was a monk for a time."

"You're not selling Twickley to me, are you?"

The age of tolerance was over. Whose religious principles would win out? I smiled: "I can't guarantee a job for you. We struggle to give our lives meaning. Bringing *you* in will frustrate that even more." I sighed. "I have no idea how you cope with those limeys at that boarding school of yours."

"*You* know what a scholarship looks like. You didn't *need* it anyway—"

"No one *needs* scholarships—people earn them. I earned mine and you earned nothing."

"That's stupid." Goro was getting harder to take seriously.

"You want to know what's *not* stupid?" I asked. "Shared joy without sex. I doubt Nietzsche admitted that second part but it doesn't make what he said any *less* stupid. What is *really* stupid is *total good*. Why should what is *morally good* rest upon its relation to human existence and its purpose in life? That seems a bit vague to me. It would not be stupid, however, if you were to join our department."

"I like power too much. Head of English? Cheltenham College? I'm powerful here."

"You have made mistakes."

The whole of Japan was in a state of civil war when Francis Xavier arrived there. He had as much influence on what people thought as the Emperor did.

Meanwhile, Goro was about to do the same. The myriad spheres of criticism that compose the humanities are the battlegrounds for civil war necessitated by the type of thinking that goes on. Goro was poised to pick up a weapon and join the fight.

"If we are going to talk about marriage, Nakadai, I would prefer to speak in Japanese."

"*Nihongo ga sukoshi shika hanasenai.*"

"What do you mean you can only speak a little? It's not like *you* to run away from words."

I closed my mind. I tried to shield my thoughts from Professor Mutton and the Great Word. "I would like to run away from this place," I admitted. "I have been here too long."

"Then leave. Get a new posting somewhere."

"It's not that simple I'm afraid. There are a few loose ends here. I would have to tie them up."

There was a long pause.

"I would like *you* to be my *partner in sin*," I explained. "Do you know how that works?"

The way Goro spoke was extra-long: "Nope."

"There are many ways you can share sin. You can cause me, or incite me, to do wrong. You can approve a wrong of mine by counsel; command; consent; provocation; praise or flattery; concealment; you can be an *active* partner in the wrongdoing. You can be silent. You can *defend* the wrong I have done."

I could hear Goro lick his lips. "It's not a student, is it?"

"What?"

"Never mind." He was thinking. "What about love?"

Some slightly more intelligent monks had asked Abbott Cooney the same thing at Burton Abbey. "Love is there *too*," I answered.

"Do you think love is part of some larger equation? Do you think it's fixed and larger than speech, language, communication?" He sighed. "I suppose I will have to ask Betty and Danielle about that—now that they're having drinks after work together where they talk about my failings as husband *and* lover. I think if love *really* existed then God wouldn't have left us to rot on this stinking planet. And who do *you* share joy with?"

"No one at current," I replied. "I once gave someone a lot of compassion. It didn't get me anywhere. But I would *love* for you to start here as soon as possible. I'll pull a few strings."

Goro said, "I look forward to seeing what strings pull you..."

The tale did not endeth here but would begin with Saito being brought on as an Assistant Lecturer in Language, Cognition & Neuroscience. Meanwhile, Nakadai became a senior lecturer in Neo-Linguistics; a pay rise which demonstrated covertly to Mutton that Nakadai was getting closer to building the Word Machine.

It is comforting to think that Saito and Nakadai comforted each other during their doctoral studies all those years ago. In contrast, I cannot say that I have been overwhelmingly comforted. Doubtless, some would say I did not undertake a PhD for comfort, and I would agree with this wholeheartedly.

What comforts me is not the occasional word of goodwill from a fellow student or colleague; on the other hand, the malaise we face is much deeper. What I found during my doctoral studies was a staggering deficiency of values; no one seemed to believe in anything. It is true, as Professor Duni Mwangangi once said, that those in the humanities—especially in linguistic-philosophical realms—have lost sight of purposeful research, and life, therefore. They have no discipline, in other words; or rather they exert discipline in the wrong areas and at the wrong time. This spreads by way of example to PhD students who, as I have seen, have the most incredible ability to belittle, depreciate and trivialize. I cannot take most of them seriously; then again, neither can they themselves. Stravinsky, or whatever his name was, for example, could hardly be described as a *serious* man...

I write these words not in defence of myself; but rather in some attempt to understand my surroundings which, as far as I can see, is an action that people like Stravinsky cannot perform.

But the truth is that I am content. I have my *Hunt Quartet* in the mornings, my series of eighteenth-century compositions written in the *Galant style* in the afternoon and then Frans Brüggen's avant-garde group, *Sourcream*, in the evening-time. I have come to terms with my impending death. The fact that human beings live only for a short time does not bother me. I might go blind or deaf, but there is nothing that cannot be dealt with through acceptance.

For example, on the note of *Divorce*, it is fascinating how Nakadai, despite his all-encompassing psychological dealings with Mutton and the Great Word, repeatedly zeroes in on the little things in life as though despite their regional unhappiness and ordinary temporal stature they were indicative of what mattered in life. Was this why he badgered Saito about his failed marriage? Whether we can answer this depends upon the input of the tall and sober man himself. But Saito, being tight-lipped, has no interest in sinking ships. Therefore, we must continue our narrative in ignorance which is what the puckish underhand Nakadai would wish us to do.

10

MUTTON PLEASED—NAKADAI DISPLEASED—PARANOIA

Professor Mutton was pleased and carried himself like the organist Alfred Hollins on his return from Australia—putting to one side how Hollins was *blind*, of course...

Nakadai had published his first book, *Translations*, which was a chunky tome in which linguistics was re-defined via an examination of Nakadai's scatter-brained diary entries written during the Tsushima War. The book garnered acclaim for Nakadai and his department as a whole. But that was not *why* Mutton behaved as though he had composed *Where I'm Coming From*, *Music of my Mind* and *Talking Book* in a few days; thus far surpassing Stevie Wonder's actual composition which took place over that impressive 3-year period. On the contrary, Mutton was most pleased because *Translations* represented ideas and hypotheses which would inform Nakadai's construction of the Word Machine and gain Mutton's master an entrance into our world.

Nakadai knew that his book of questions would quite possibly lead to the destruction of the planet. He persisted, however, with the exercise to the extent that he permitted Mutton to contact his master to describe what the book contained. All of this, the entirety of the operation, was carried out in the utmost secrecy. (Much like the unprovable involvement of Jean Cocteau in the murder of Erik Satie, nobody knew the darker purpose of the Neo-Linguistic project.) Nakadai relayed to me the pressure he faced to deliver the Great Word's nefarious doorway as well as helpful lectures and seminars for students and relevant advice for his postgraduates, one of which, in due course, would be me:

> Maybe I was being punished for everything I had done wrong. I have done *considerable* wrong but who hasn't? It is impossible to live and *not* commit wrongdoing and sin. I miss female company. Having lost my mother and Ms. Chiba, the women I used to look up to, I have been without female company for a long time. My failure to foster relationships with women *has* been a major sin. Buddhism, for example, views obsession and earthly passion with hostility. I have always found the trick in Catholicism is to temper those obsessions and passions; to make them work for me and not against me. The postgraduate students I have supervised over the years have been men, mostly. However, this maybe says more about the university than me. I have enjoyed your company immensely, Nicola—and what is wrong saying I have done so because you *are* a woman? Many will hate me for this but I like women because they *are* women. In the name of God, Nicola, is there nothing to be gained from platonic attachment and shared joy and warmth?

The benefits are brief and powerful when a man and a woman commiserate like *siblings*. One sees the other through themselves. And the other does the same. Today everyone is terrified of shared joy and warmth. They are frightened to death of temporary siblings who dominate and guide them. Is there nothing to be gained from Platonic attachment and shared joy and warmth? The hope of these interactions *binds* the sexes. They are strong together and weak apart. Expedience overrules understanding when men and women cease to learn from each other. Advantageousness *cancels* self-sacrifice and altruism. Then there is the daily grind. I have Professor Mutton and the Great Word to contend with. Do the powers *they* represent go beyond gender? When *Translations*, my first book, filled the local Waterstones with enthusiastic Neo-Linguistic followers, was the shared joy and warmth between men and women there as well? I do not know. What I do know is that I *hated* Professor Mutton and the Great Word because they got between me and you. They made any Platonic attachment impossible and I grew bitter and resentful, not at them, but at *you*...and *that* is evil...

Ernst Hoffman, whose fantasy stories greatly influenced Wagner, would often pace his apartment when writing his review of Beethoven's latest compositions. He would send his friends away and suck on lemons. This extreme pressure on Nakadai to deliver research about the construction of a faultless Word Machine, by way of comparison, led to his lashing out at those closest to him. Without his knowledge, a flattering remark had been supplied to his publisher, Oakley Books, to place on the front cover of *Translations*.

The quote, which sadly could not replicate the pinnacle of perception as illustrated by Hoffman's writings on Beethoven, claimed that *Translations* was "consistent, sacred, positively loaded with wisdom and totally profound". This did not improve Nakadai's mood as it reminded him of the Tsushima War. Memories of dying soldiers and wooden planks flooded his already frantic and panicked mind.

> The Great Word and I had a kind of *sacred history*. Who knew where it began and ended? I may never have shaken off its control during the Tsushima War. There was a possibility that it had waited. I was becoming the New Testament of myself and there was something more powerful about me. I was greater in failure than anything else...

There was only one man who could have supplied that flattering remark and Nakadai opted to call him on the internal line—despite how Saito's office was but a single leap down the hallway. With that in mind, it becomes necessary for our narrative to include the following memoirish text.

> The Second Japanese Intelligence Department is bugging my office. What proof do I have? None whatsoever. It is something I would like to *think* is true but truth and thinking have little in common. They do not feed into one another as the masculine and the feminine do. Together, truth and thought are

like a *world without end*. If I shall continue to praise God in heaven with my prayers then *why* must I pray now? There is nothing in the world that is true because some pauper thought it through; less so when a thinker does the thinking. I think of Goro when I need someone to fit *that* description: the man who thought harder than the pauper and failed *twice* as religiously. (Why do I feel as though I am describing myself?) He recently supplied a quote to my publisher. They wanted something flattering to put on the cover and he gave it to them.

I lost my head when the book was published; when I saw his words emblazoned on the cover. I called him on the internal line and threatened to kill him.

"Who is that?" he asked.

"You know *damn* well who it is! Nakadai, Nakadai, Nakadai!

"You are just down the hall though—"

"That comment is one hundred percent without merit. I want to know what the bloody hell you thought you were doing when you gave that quote to my publisher?"

"The quote for *Translations*?"

"You little poo. Yes, the quote you gave them—the one about *Translations* being "consistent" and 'sacred" and all that crap."

"What about it?" he asked sheepishly.

"Must I—oh boy—must I write everything in the spiky rubric? Yes! That is *precisely* what I am talking about! With God as my witness!"

Doubtless, Goro considered why our most tantalizing discussions were held over the phone, much in the same way King Herod held all those babies. "Well, your publisher asked me for a blurb. I gave it to them. I had *nothing* to do with that awful Arial font, though; I had *zero* input on that decision."

"The font is not the issue!" I thundered down the line. "What *does* matter is you can't be certain about my book being either *consistent* or *sacred*! You have thrown me under the bus!"

One of my less intelligent postgraduate students walked into my office. "Hey, Nakadai."

I was horrified. "Did you read the sign on my door?"

"What sign? Is this a *test*?"

"There is a sign on my door which says, *Knock, then wait, like a pleasant pineapple*. You didn't see that?"

"What do those signs *indicate* though? That's the question *par excellence*. I'm doing Neo-Linguistics. Do you like it?"

"Certainly not! Now sod off!" They followed my instructions and I returned to shouting at Goro. "Sorry about that, Goro. Where was I? You've thrown me under the bus! I shouldn't be surprised given your track record."

"What does *that* mean?"

"I wrote *Translations* during the Tsushima War—a war you did *not* take part in!"

Down the hall, I heard the door slam. Footsteps beat their way up to mine. The door opened and Goro stared me down. "Listen to me—"

"There is a sign on my door which says, *Knock, then wait, like a pleasant—*"

"Listen to me you *warugaki*. You keep your nose out of my business. Do you understand?"

"Shut the door! For God's sake!"

Goro shut the door. We were alone. "Have you *any* idea what I did to keep out of that stupid war? And you go gallivanting off like some *daimyo* into another parish. Why did you do it?"

I stirred. "I had no choice. My aunt was busy running an Asian Supermarket in Twickley whilst *yours* was sending young Japanese to their deaths."

"How *dare* you. How *dare* you compare me to my family."

"What do you mean?"

"I am *not* my family. I am Goro Saito and I came here at your request and...you treat me *this* way?" He was huge standing over me. Generosity had lent him the will of God. "What do you *want*, Nakadai?"

"I want to learn from my mistakes."

"I don't believe you."

"It's true. I want to learn from my mistakes, and live, and scream out—" The office grew dark in the same way the cathedral had that fateful day. That same altered reality had wormed its way to my office.

"I am warning you," the Great Word whispered, "you will not speak about me—if you do, I will *penalize* you!" I gripped my chest as the room returned to normal. I could see Goro watching me irritated. "What are you doing *now*?" he asked.

"I'm sorry..."

"Nakadai? What's wrong with you?"

"No, it's just—I'm *tired*. I am just trying to get my breath back. Think of the time one spends getting one's breath back! What a waste of time!"

"Well, I hope you learn from your mistakes," Goro admonished, "you ungrateful *bastard*..."

I was relieved when he stormed out. I realized my mind was not unique. No matter where I was, when I was, the Great Word could *find* me. The same vindictive, curious influence that had gripped Professor Mutton was now gripping me—it was strong and undefeated...

I find it worrying that, despite my studying in the realm of theoretical and applied linguistics, I find it difficult to describe how I feel about the fictionalization above. It is characteristic clandestine material that I struggle to read as though I were gaping through the bathroom window of Pietro Mascagni during the composition of one of his more *realistic* operas. Perhaps it is because I knew Nakadai personally that I bear such torment at the prospect and exercise of being afforded the double-edged privilege of studying his rich and terrifying history. When I walk around campus, I feel that *nothing* is being done; that will be *my* terrifying history.

11

DREAM—JAPAN—PROFESSORSHIP

I had a dream shortly before I returned to Japan. The year is 1596 and I am being taken to the town of Banbayama in Gifu Prefecture. I am tied to the back of a horse, and the horse is being led through the surrounding forest by the *bakafu*; the police in those days. They stop the horse just outside the town. They untie me and walk me into the square. There is a crowd but they are silent. Samurai Kenzou Hiroshi exits an administrative building. I can sense he's related to me, but he looks at me scornfully. "*Anata wa kyūkyoku no fujunbutsu o motte imasu!*" I have the *ultimate impurity*, which I assume is Christianity but could also be homosexuality. "*Iesu Kirisuto was shinde imasu! Kare ni kuwawariaidesu ka?*" Jesus Christ is dead. He asks me if I want to join him. He does not allow me to answer any of these questions, however, and I find myself despairing about what will happen next. "*Mearī wa baishunpudeshita!*" Whether Mary Magdalene was a prostitute is still up for debate. What is wrong is thinking there is something *shameful* about prostitution, in my opinion. *"Yuda wa tadashikatta!"* Whether Judas was right or wrong has no bearing on the will of God; I know that is true. For a time, I hear the pitter-patter of peasants' feet. Finally, Kenzou Hiroshi, my ancestor, orders his bakafu to lay me on a pre-prepared cross. They raise a hammer and nail over my right hand. And that is the end of the dream. I remember waking up and regretting accepting the invitation from the Tokyo Media School. They had asked me to give a visiting lecture. I quickly accepted the offer. I remember thinking I should have spent more time thinking about the offer. But so much time is wasted like this. I would not alter my decision. I would do what I said I would do, and endeavour to learn from my mistakes...

Nakadai ought to have the fullest sensorial vocabulary possible here. I will not make any further remarks, then, until the uncovered memoirish text that follows is terminated by its atypical, intricate author.

I was 49 when I returned to Japan. I hoped to stay as far away as possible from the Yamanashi Sanatorium. I had bad memories of that place and did not want to remember it. My journey started at Manchester Airport, however, which was *just* as bad. I boarded the flight with a change of clothes and a collection of short stories by Eiko Egami. When meeting an author for the first time it's not a bad idea to read their work. I had a paperback edition; the cover was a reproduction of a painting by Hieronymus Bosch. I cracked it open to the first page when the plane took off. The title of the first (and longest) story was *Philosophy of Burden*. I found it compelling and terrifying. It was a bold and stupid story and its humanity was stained. In the absence of any specific law, Egami could only be *fair*. And that was what she had written in her story. I had just enough time to translate the story into English. I wrote as quickly as I could and have included my translation of *Philosophy of Burden* below.

PHILOSOPHY OF BURDEN

Written under duress by Dr. Eiko Egami
Translated from Japanese by Hiroshi Nakadai

I woke up at 3:00 a.m. the other day and my mind was in a buzzing relentless mood, so I got up to use the toilet as I usually do at 3:00 a.m., only to find that my endless agitation was unaffected by my quiet pissing. I could not sleep. I have found it very difficult to sleep recently. I have always found sleep trying.

When I was young my parents were unhappy because they lived between two noisy houses in which our relatives lived and because they were our relatives felt they had some kind of impunity when it came to noise pollution. Bastards. I don't remember whether or not I was able to sleep when I was young.

When I was at boarding school, I always had nightmares about wanting to get out and there being ghosts in my boarding house, girls who had never left, so to speak. Again, I can't remember how well I slept at boarding school. Whilst I was there, I wanted to take a flamethrower to the school and many of the people who worked at or attended the school.

Then, when I was at the Tokyo Media School doing my BA, I barely slept because I was drunk. I don't remember any of that if I can be honest, apart from one blowjob which ended with me gagging and vomiting—I hate how we pretend that that doesn't happen. That doesn't mean I don't enjoy giving blowjobs; only that there are risks involved.

After that, I did my PhD at the University of Twickley and slept a lot because I was doing a doctorate in English Literature and my thesis was on Dostoyevsky via Žižek and I needed as much sleep as I could get. Now I have a shitty office in the Humanities building at the University of Ibigawa which is a terrible university. We barely register in the rankings. Most of my colleagues barely register when I'm in my shitty office. My surroundings blend into a social pudding and I scrape my spoon across the upper layers to see if it's worth eating.

I've gradually been losing sleep, patience and love. Without these things, you might as well kill yourself.

When I walk on the street there are multitudes, armies of citizens I would like to kill because they are citizens and not human beings, precisely. I've been developing a philosophy of my own—and *personal philosophies* are either hated or used incorrectly and kept a secret because normal people loathe the idea that other people have *thoughts*—a philosophy of my own that comes down to facts and matter. The fact of the matter is that matter is fact, that facts are proofs, that proof can be verified, that verification can be monitored, that monitoring is subjective, that subjectivity is singular, that singularities are categorized, that categorization is biased, that biases are prejudiced, that prejudice is counterfeit and that counterfeits are realistic.

Then, we need to see that reality is visual, that sight is constant, that consistencies are regulated, that regulation is forced, that force is planned, that planning is premeditated, that premeditation is essential, that essentials are prioritized, that prioritization is organized, that organization is systematic, that systems are limited, that limits can be verified, that verification is proof, that proofs are facts, and that fact is matter—*quod erat demonstrandum*.

As for those who want to talk about metaphysics and language, I hope they all die in a violent car crash, one of those where you can barely recognise the car afterwards. I want to say, "I'm a genius, a person of unbelievable intelligence, a woman of dearest positive insight, a radiant star, a beam of versatility and flexibility," except it wouldn't be true. There aren't any bona fide geniuses any more than there are bona fide social workers, and teachers. We'd like to speak of there being a *sine qua non* for every one of our precious orthodox distinctions but in reality, there are no requirements. I also want to ask myself, "Is it bad that I sometimes want to scream?" but what prevents me from doing such a stupid thing—the asking, not the screaming—is that I instinctively know it's bad of me. But I don't care anymore. I've lost my sleep, my patience, my love; and the most important of these three is *love*.

What would a *God* do with love, patience and sleep? He would fritter it away making absurd worlds in which absurd fauna lived under the absurd canopies of absurd flora. Free time is both a crime and a punishment. I would much prefer it if every God—were they to exist—could happily toss away their love, patience, sleep, and shuffle elsewhere with their frivolous and unthinking ideas. If the lineage of sight always returns me to matter, then I don't need a God to create the circumstances in which an existential crisis lifts me to a higher plain of appreciation—It is the notion of a lack of appreciation that is so disgusting because it suggests that I am in the wrong whenever I am dissatisfied with my world.

Only a lunatic with a degree from the lowest-ranked university on the planet could be satisfied with the world in which we find ourselves. Years ago, we were given the greatest pedagogical tool in the history of mankind in the form of the Internet. It is not the case that our forefathers and foremothers did *not* pack the web with information and knowledge and wisdom. The awful truth is that the human race has decided to ignore it in favour of sucking, fucking, breasts, penises, testicles, vaginas, biceps, buttocks and rape ranging from the decidedly mild to the decidedly evil.

I am a woman, but I do not care that I am a woman. The discrepancy between my existential self and my gender is an enormous one. If I had focused on my gender as many other people ridiculously do, I would have been a *dead* woman a long time ago. This is what I say: if being a hater of men means that I hate with inveterate venom all men who take it upon themselves to conduct an affront to my genius, then yes, I hate all men! And if being misogynistic means that I despise all women who foolishly take it upon themselves to discredit my absolute supremacy, then yes, I am misogynistic! And if all the inhabitants of the world in their infinitely *non compos mentis* countries collectively agree to shout down my claim to the ultimate mental agility—which I rightly deserve—then yes, I detest all human life! I condemn it to the indolence and inactivity wrought from sleep, the befuddlement and uncertainty received from patience, the flaws and decrepitudes squeezed from the fruit of love.

"You're a monster!" you want to shout; "You have no morality!" If you were able to distinguish a human being from a monster; if you were able to geographically mark out good from evil on a map of the human mind, you would be the wisest person to have ever walked the earth. But as of today, you are not. There is no potential for evil within people; there is only evil. There is no potential for good that seeps through the thin skin of good-willed people; there is only avarice, hate and intolerance. I find *that* good. "What do you believe?" you will ask; "I bet you have a list of things, a dogma you adhere to, on your smartphone, or a notebook in your back pocket!" What I believe is this:

Matter is fact.
Facts are proofs.
Proof can be verified.
Verification can be monitored.
Monitoring is subjective.
Subjectivity is singular.
Singularities are categorized.
Categorization is biased.
Biases are prejudiced.
Prejudice is counterfeit.
Counterfeits are realistic.
Reality is visual.
Sight is constant.
Consistencies are regulated.

Regulation is forced.
Force is planned.
Planning is premeditated.
Premeditation is essential.
Essentials are prioritized.
Prioritization is organized.
Organization is systematic.
Systems are limited.
Limits can be verified.
Verification is proof.
Proofs are facts.
Fact is matter.

The previous section in which I outlined my beliefs in no way represents me. The ideas are badly thought out and misrepresent the deepest feelings of my psyche. But a damaged MacBook must still have been a functioning computer at one point. Thus, I will not apologise for the previous section because to do that would be to say that I was *totally* wrong in my self-assessment. The fact that I'm breathing demonstrates that what I said made at least a little bit of sense and was at least a little representative of the state of my brain.

Where my misgivings would be inaccurate, however, would be in my saying that I have never been afraid. I'm not afraid to say that I have been afraid in the past; I will be afraid in the future at some point as well. Just the other day, Betty, one of the less intelligent students in my Introduction to Western Literature course, emailed me to organise a face-to-face meeting to discuss her future. I can't describe my fury and discontent with the email that I received, the potential monotonous torture that would consist of sitting down with this subpar student, this lowlife, this stinking pile of useless fatty tissue, and discussing what might or might not be distressing her about the course—or in general! At the same time, I was petrified of accountability, scared stiff from what would be the relentless reality of her spotty unattractive face, and mercilessly self-loathing at the prospect of lowering myself to her pond scum level of existence.

The following day she came into my office. I gave her the usual polite bullshit which is part and parcel of the University-tutor mantra. She then proceeded to describe her addled unhealthy frame of mind, her various eating disorders, her expensive medications, her love of the human spirit that she so often encountered on campus, but also the deep depression into which she had fallen *as a direct result of her enrolling on my course*. She did not know how William Shakespeare could have brought himself to write about a black man. She found the pious poetry of George Herbert to be offensive and naïve. She was confused as to why I had labelled Mr. Micawber from *David Copperfield* a wastrel and disastrous human being who needed nothing more than immediate execution at the expense of the state.

Nor did Betty understand why James Baldwin's *Giovanni's Room* was a masterpiece because it scrutinized human beings under an overbearing microscope. She also thought that Erika in Elfriede Jelinek's *The Piano Teacher* was a victim and that Toni Morrison was a modern-day fascist and bigot. She then explained to me that she had thought about committing suicide many times, had tried to commit suicide at least twice during the course of the term, then said that I was her only hope of regaining any kind of sanity. Needless to say, I had nothing constructive to say to her apart from: "I think you should contact University services."

"Why?" she was offended. "So, I can get laughed at? Is *that* why you want me to get in touch with the University's services? All those trouser stains will do is scrutinise me a little harder than you have and then tell me to take my medication and that life is rougher than I thought it would be."

Immediately I was struck by Betty's open-minded remark. It seemed to me that she was somebody who had given away her sleep, her patience, her love...I was looking at myself...At the same time, I hated her as much as any other person I'd ever met; I thought she was hideous, badly measured, hopelessly out of her depth, a loathsome mushroom in the Black Forest of life. I told her that I had weighed up her options for some time now and that Betty's best course of action would be to become a porn star, preferably one with no standards which would mean that she would make a lot more money than other porn stars. She would be the greatest starlet who ever lived.

Betty was not amused, she thought I was joking. "What did you just say to me?" How many times must a human being be faced with the truth until they understand that humour and humility and patience are mere by-products of truth and horror and those disgusting pimples of decisions that daily western existence consists of between the ads on YouTube and the loveless forums on Facebook? "Are you deaf as well?" I asked; "I'm being deadly serious when I tell you that your best course of action is to become a porn star. I've never been more serious in all my life. You're one of the lucky ones. Do you know how many students I meet every year? And out of these students, have you any idea of the number of individuals enrolled at this University who would be doing themselves a favour if they were to immediately drop out, start a pornographic Instagram page, get themselves an agent at an adult entertainment agency in Los Angeles and become a full-time porn star? These people are so ill-suited to life, so hopelessly emotionally inadequate—*not physically gifted but physically inclined*—that the world would benefit if they were to perform coitus at least 4 times a day in front of a film crew who do not love them but want their body, and the money that body generates. *You, Betty, are one of these sorry lucky many.* Even now as we speak, in your year there are at least 20 people who would be doing themselves a favour by cutting their ties with the University and myself completely and setting up a camera at home and filming themselves either on their own or with other people doing monstrously degrading and endlessly titillating things with their bodies. I've seen documentaries about these people, these starlets. They trick themselves into believing that they are attractive and are doing something of worth; they fool themselves into thinking that their personalities are valued by the people who exploit them. I'm of the opinion that a second-rate slave is one who gets paid. And that is what you would be: a second-rate slave. Yet are they without value? No! Even if you subject yourself to this reprehensible exploitation, you will still have more value than those mothers who prioritise their careers over their children. Those people have no souls, I fear; but with 10 to 20 successful videos on Pornhub or XHamster, you would not only have your soul but also several thousand dollars in your bank account, a future career, equally degraded comrades, an endless line of sexually immature boyfriends and girlfriends who cannot tell the difference between a good fuck and that worrisome powerful itch we've decided in our faulty wisdom to call love. *You have no love, no patience, no sleep, I can understand why*—but that is no reason to throw your life away at this juncture, to continue on a course (no pun intended) where you are destined to feel pea-brained, impotent, deformed, taciturn, thick-skulled, meagre and inferior, an underachieving vanquished dead loss of an idiot..."

I remember her face swelled up in sorrow and she began to cry relentlessly. She stood up convulsing and shook her hands as if they were on fire. Then she gripped her face as though she wished to tear it off and replace it with mine—she swung open the door, and ran into the corridor, her naïve ravings turning the once unbelievably dull departmental area into a carnival of excess and terror.

But that is just one example from my comparatively short career in academia. I have lived an empty pathetic life, a pointless life, a life with little to no danger. So, you can imagine my glee when during one of my seminars for my Introduction to Western Literature course—I recall it was my devastating seminar on the equilibrium of Jelinek's *The Piano Teacher*—when I was attempting to explain why Walter Klemmer admires Norman Mailer as an artist a poorly little student by the name of Arthur Wandought began to rub his head as though he was suffering from a mixture of intense fear and nausea. Then he tried to answer one of my questions and came across as totally simple, mentally deranged, after which he lost control of his muscles and his body flung itself all over the place and he smacked his lips and convulsed whilst he sucked for air. During this terrifying event, he fouled himself. The smell was detrimental to the lesson. He crumpled into a human heap of hardly recognisable exhaustion and anxiety.

During Arthur's epileptic fit several of my students including Betty looked to me for common-sensical guidance, but I could offer none whatsoever as I was transfixed by the kinetic monstrosity before me. This poor, tiny, pale and underfed Arthur Wandought personified my lack of sleep, patience and love. He never broke his gaze with mine, it was an intimate process. His affliction and my observation, his wretchedness and my vacant voyeuristic examination of his convulsing body. I was so pleased with it! It was not aesthetically pleasing but it was existentially pleasing because something was happening that was out of my control. My satisfaction quickly turned into outright joy as the intensity of Arthur's suffering reduced and he returned to a vegetable-like state. His fellow students looked on as though he were a lump of poorly butchered meat in a supermarket. And it was during that time that I believed his fellow students to be reprehensible and stupid. I took advantage of the situation to appear as though I cared about that poor and pale Arthur Wandought when in reality, he was perhaps the least successful on my list of students. He did not have the privilege of being able to undertake a successful career in pornography. He was less than that. He was not even a good failure. I nonetheless paid a great deal of attention in my thoughts to that event for the rest of the week. I cogitated upon it frequently and often found myself at the centre of this emotionless pitiful empathy web.

But, again, that is just one example from my relatively brief and useless career. I can barely bring myself to call my life a career as it bears more resemblance to an all-out war. I don't think military generals, for example, have careers: what they have is an agenda of prolonged homicide, which, now that I think about it, is probably the equivalent of what my life will consist of when I die. I say "will probably consist of" because human beings tend to engage in that disgusting pastime of judging and evaluating the lives of people who are no longer living. We call it an act of remembrance when in fact we would be doing ourselves a great favour if we were to forget about the majority of people who die either in their sleep or under grisly depraved circumstances. This is what many would call an opinion. It is true then that subjectivity is singular and that it always becomes clear that fact is matter. And all a dead body is, is matter.

Several weeks ago, I had the unfortunate privilege of being invited to give a eulogy at the funeral of a wastrel and loser by the name of Toshiro. He had been in and out of many jobs throughout his short life and had managed to be fired from all of them. He had had great promise in his youth for the reason that he was remarkably intelligent, pensive and empathetic. But these positive attributes soon gave way to stupidity, passion and arrogance, and a sublime loathing of the world exterior to his brain. I submit that I was embarrassed about our friendship. Every couple of years, it seemed, our friendship would be renewed through a pathetic message sent on Facebook, a dribbling mewling phone call in the middle of the day, or a passive-aggressive email sent in the early hours of the morning and usually under the influence of alcohol. I cannot name the reason I gave in to these revolting invitations, but it seemed that the reason was always strong, mysterious and deep within me. I would spend an hour or so listening to his strange monologues about the pulsive state of his life, how he could not find a job, how his family refused to speak with him, how every human being he had ever come into contact with and sympathised with had always proceeded to fail him or punish him for no reason whatsoever. And Toshiro was so innately pathetic and apparently without value that it became impossible not to believe him—it was logically impossible for him to be dishonest.

Remarkably, I found myself invited to the funeral. I did not want to give a eulogy, but I was made to do so, nonetheless. His family, other friends and I were ushered into this ancient decrepit church in some quiet quarter of the city and were subsequently tortured by the vain shallow words of the priest and the overall decadence and dishonesty of the entire service.

Eventually, the time came for me to ascend the pulpit. My heels thudded across the rich burgundy carpet and I felt queasy and uncomfortable as I looked upon so many tawdry faces who seemed to pierce my flesh as I fumbled about with my speech. I began:

"Family, friends...and I see a few enemies. We'd be fooling ourselves if we were to have such a massive gathering and not suffer the presence of enemies in our midst." There was nervous gasping at this remark, but I did not care: "I knew Toshiro for a long time. Our friendship seemed to be renewed biannually, usually in one of those seedy saké bars across the road in which Toshiro was an almost constant presence. I must confess that we were not so close as we had been towards the end. I detested his empty prattling monologues about the vagrant state of his sorry life, and he detested my fervent iconoclastic raving. But there was always an invisible reason as to why we continued to fraternise with one another. I think the reason was love; not a love of the romantic sort but a love of the kind that is so often spoken of in the great religions. Love that for many people is almost impossible to comprehend. Love that is pure and powerful. Regardless of any kind of love, however, I am of the mind that Toshiro died alone and, in a shivering, melancholic state with all of his money having been spent and with his apartment in a truly grotesque state of disarray with unclean dishes in the corner of the filthy kitchenette and soiled laundry pouring out of the second-hand washing machine that was seldom activated. Ladies and gentlemen, it is safe to say that our departed family member and friend died at rock bottom. But he never robbed anyone; he never raped or killed anyone; on his death bed, his accounts were a clean state of affairs. He owed no money. And yet, ladies and gentlemen, were his family, his friends, his enemies, indeed, at his beck and call in his time of need? They were not. I am included in these groups. When you have sunk so low to new levels of depravity even an enemy is welcome, but there would not even be an enemy present at the moment of Toshiro's unfortunate demise. He died alone in great pain on an unmade bed stained with addictive substances from store-bought bottles. When I heard about his passing, I was frightened, angry, shocked and embittered. But I know for a fact that none of you in this room so much as flinched when you were told about Toshiro's untimely death. Everyone in this room has failed Toshiro throughout his entire life and terminally. That is what we do in this country, we set up our young people for failure early on and revel in their often-peculiar self-destruction. Toshiro was a failure of a human being because we made him a failure and wanted him to crumble. Any possibility that he might be employed we regarded with disgust; any hope that he would find true love in this world we felt an aversion towards; any chance that he might find potatoes to make his cheap croquettes, which so often was the only food he could afford, we found intolerable and sabotaged at every opportunity. We may be in a holy place, but our presence makes it sacrilegious to the values this building represents. We are hellhounds, savages, barbarians, devils. We will surely go to hell because in truth none of us care about Toshiro, even today!" There was more gasping and cursing but I was on a roll: "When we leave this building today and return to our stupid lives, we will be none the wiser. None of us have even the most rudimentary comprehension of life, nature or the known universe! We are content to pass through this place in black garments and to sit our overfed asses on these monstrously uncomfortable benches nodding our heads like idiots; we will go home like idiots!"

"Boooooo!" some blockhead of a relative shouted from the back pews.

"And I congratulate you on being the first person in this fine city of ours to *boo* a eulogy!" I retorted. "Spare us your petty insults, you infamous moron! The truth is that I do not feel even the least bit insulted as all *you* have managed in your unseemly outburst is to insult Toshiro and his memory. You will surely be unremembered, Sir! Do you want to know what I think? I think you have always wanted to insult Toshiro, but that you never dared to do so until the man himself was dead! How *dare* you take an opportunity for revenge at a funeral; you worm!

Parasite! As for the rest of this screwy unintelligent crowd, I can only assume that you too wanted to insult Toshiro and his memory, except you were so selfish and bored out of your minds by the proceedings that you decided that such an unseemly outburst would be a waste of hot breath! Nobody in this room is a friend to the deceased. Let that be today's lesson. Throughout Toshiro's life, you were all nothing but treacherous, self-serving, difficult and malignant apparitions in an otherwise unharming life! And given that many of you managed to turn up today demonstrates that you are either divinely stupid or have the privilege to suffer inordinate amounts of bravery! Remember this, too: if God were real, he would surely strike all of us down in this room, loathsome idiots that we are!" There was suddenly an outpouring of slights and slanders from the funereal crowd. I quickly gathered myself and snuck out of the church. I managed to evade the many family members, friends and enemies who were wishing death upon me at an alarming rate. But not once did I ever feel guilty about what I did and the whole experience confirmed to me my spiritual perfection and unspoiled genius for scrupulousness. I had loved those people and had been rejected.

The hardest people to love are those who donate money to so-called charitable causes. "How can you be lower than a dog?" you may say. But I respect dogs immensely and would never call another human being a dog to imply that they were indicative of a low existence. No, that would be much too cruel on my part; and cruelty was never the basis for any reality *par excellence*. You may ask me, "Where is the cruelty in the world?" and I shall reply: the cruelties lay in those devilish deeds that are passed off as good ones. Much more than that, it is not the deed so much as it is the person who benefits spiritually and *brings that spirit forward with them*. If you commit the ultimate barbarity, e.g., strangling with your bare hands a dog that is attacking a baby, and think yourself charitable and decent and do *not* bring such sentiments forward to apply them to *other more pertinent situations*, then you have merely committed folly. You might as well have strangled the child. Better still, strangle the child and train the dog to protect you. And if the dog cannot be trained then let yourself sink into the pit of humility and leave the dog alone, let it make its way. "Ah, but you don't let the baby make its way!" That is true and look where saving the stupid child got us in the first place—Whence does the desire to be upstanding derive from? A woman could strangle all the dogs and children in the world and some dolt would still think her to be an upstanding decent individual! The point is not that that dolt would be mistaken, but that it is useless categorising human beings into good columns and bad columns at all. They are all doomed. And it's of no help whatsoever to introduce prejudice into doom.

All that preceded is nothing but unsubstantiated gossip, however. This is the closest I have ever gotten to thinking I am a fool. Yet I understand that if I were to think myself an idiot, I would be wrong. It is so difficult to get yourself across to other people, to define your character and make sense for an audience the desire for often negative ramifications in your life. "If you behaved yourself there would be no negative ramifications," you declare. In a world where positive ramifications do not exist, that declaration is feckless and selfish. It is feckless because it supposes that the end of all life is not death but more life, and it is selfish because it seeks to undermine the lives of others when without a doubt the speaker is a most contaminated and lowly individual. How could such a person make a correct judgement of anything? That is why when I remark that my Head of Department Professor Mifune is lower than pond scum in his intellectualism, I am not making a spurious judgement but declaring a logical fact of matter. Spend 10 minutes with him and you will see that I am right. Spend 5 minutes with the rest of humanity and you will see how lowly, pathetic and selfish *they* all are. These are the facts, and it would be wrong of me *not* to voice them each day for those willing barbarians to hear.

"But these are just words," anyone will say. "What we want are physical examples!" And you shall have them. One is all I need. Without sleep, you cannot think. Without patience, you cannot sleep. Without love, you are lost.

After a gruelling day of two lectures and one seminar I had to give, I was more or less done with humanity and sought to return to my apartment in the city. I collected my badly thought-out notes and placed them in my ancient decrepit briefcase and made my way out of the departmental building.

As usual, I stared into every window I passed and saw a variety of mewling individuals who had not even a morsel of hope for the future. I made my way onto a pedestrian path and watched the seagulls flying overhead. I noticed a group of local 12-year-olds was approaching, all of them wearing tracksuits or hoodies. In the past, I had always ignored these derogatory creatures and looked ahead ignoring whatever foul depravities exited their mouths. This time was different. I felt a kind of fire in my belly, a complete disregard for nature and the desire to exterminate something irrevocably. As the 12-year-olds scuttled passed me the smallest child said, "Do you fancy a shag, love?" except he said it without love or affection and smeared entirely with malice and venom. What he had uttered had been a barb of animosity and bitterness and not a bud of maturity and tenderness. Filled now with indignation and wrathful thinking I quickly replied, "Fuck off..." and continued my way down the path to remove me from an otherwise silly situation.

Several seconds passed behind me and the silence was palpable until finally, the smallest child worked up the courage to demand satisfaction for what I had said to him. He was raving against the alleged injustice of my comment and was antagonistic, dyspeptic and outraged in the most hostile manner imaginable.

I had dared to do what others feigned doing. *I had shown him himself.* But I too had been provoked and was now incandescent and full of rage with this child, this child whose mother no doubt was a filthy animal deprived of dignity and gravitas—I couldn't even imagine him having a father—so with a fury that surprised even myself, I turned around and walked back towards the 12-year-olds who were now stood in the middle of the pedestrian path.

"It is true that I told you to fuck off, but you are incapable of understanding basic Japanese even though you are little more than a peasant with delusions of Samurai-grandeur flickering through your tiny mind. If you come any closer, I will exterminate you and leave your friends alive as an example of the enlightened state I leave people in after I encounter them."

But this child proved to be illiterate and moronic and incapable of understanding the implications of my frank promise to the thick-headed mound of flesh and bone that was standing before me. It was like he was waiting for something to happen: *perhaps he wanted me to kill him? All along he had planned this and would now reap his architectured consequences.* But this notion only filled me with more resentment towards the obtuse and idiotic sack of blood in front of me. I bent down to the ground and picked up a rock by the side of the road. I raised it above my head and then brought it down onto the child's forehead which cracked and squished as the creature fell forward onto the tarmac. In a response that I had anticipated the other 12-year-olds were not paralysed with fear but were inspired into rapid locomotion by their sudden hysterical comprehension of what I had done to their acquaintance. They left him and me alone on the pedestrian path. And I was alone with the act I had committed. For some reason, I placed my briefcase on the ground and leant down to inspect the boy's head. The ravine that I had cut into the skin seemed to penetrate through the bone and into the child's brain, some of which I could have sworn was spilling out onto the tarmac. I was foaming at the mouth and apoplectic as well as forlorn and humiliated. I was depressed and regretful as well as dignified in my victory and delighted at the prospect of succeeding at something.

Yes! I had succeeded! But what on Earth could success mean for a person so committed to the fact of matter as I was? What I deemed to be a favourable outcome would be deemed to be murder by the state. Where was my wealth? Where was the affluence and fortune that I had so desired in my desperation to kill the child? The answer was that the triumph was on the path in front of me and that if I did not find good reason to recognise the prosperity and dignified qualities in what I had done then quickly I would succumb to the mounting pressures around me and collapse into the Earth's crust a spiritually defined devil. This latter option was so tempting, however, that I decided to abandon any chance of excavating sagacity or logic from what I had done and to commit myself instead to the justice of those risible high-opinioned slugs who would condemn me.

At the same time, all the disquietudes of my life seemed to pour into my brain, and I began to panic about and dread the mockery of justice that would follow. This was an irrational fear. I had always known that the nightmare was all around me, that neurosis, anxieties and irrational fears were the building blocks of any human experience and existence, therefore. But there grew within me the sense that I was no longer capable of penetrating such realities. I could not demonstrate or encapsulate the horrors of the universe for other unfortunate lowly people. I could not summarise or describe the tediousness of existential nonsense that plagued only the most intelligent people. I could no longer make an ornament of my life and embellish it with tawdry immature examples and rambling misgivings that seemed only to define what I lacked as opposed to what I possessed.

I went to the train station and decided against going to Tokyo. I hated cities. Instead, I bought a ticket for a train to Ibigawa: a disgusting part of the country that less intelligent and less conniving people would no doubt avoid like the plague. I got on the train and sat next to the toilet, which constantly opened and closed because there was a faulty automatic door. The train pulled out of the station and began to make its way to its hellish destination. Unfortunately, at the same time that I had boarded the train, so, too, had a team of Transport Police who had been informed of the murder that I had committed, and were now set on capturing the alleged fiend.

I watched these three mockeries of human design swaggering down the aisle towards me. They had holsters on their belts and envy in their eyes for every passive noncommunicative passenger they traded glares with.

They finally traded glares with me because I was looking straight at them. After all, I loathe confrontation and think it ought to be confronted.

The End

Philosophy of Burden had such a profound effect on me I fainted like that unfortunate, Arthur Wandought. When I awoke the *holy nails* were piercing the backs of my eyes. I stared out the window. My plane descended between two rows of International District Hotels, a conglomerate owned by the solar panel pundit, Queen

Uliana of Algeria, whose habit of posting nude photos on Twitter sent shock throughout the world because she was a man. The hotels guaranteed diplomatic immunity for registered guests; I would be able to commit any crime I wanted during my stay, provided I did it outside the hotel. There was a powerful *neology* waiting for me there, however, and her story gave a good indication of the kind of bunkmate she would be.

My plane touched down. A 24-hour parade was ordered to operate along the runway when Japan won the Tsushima War. It had hardly been a victory; especially since the South Korean high command had come out afterwards explaining how General Chun-hei Choe had thrown a wobbly. The Japanese government rejected this *nuptial blessing*—they had their ministerial jobs to worry about.

I walked across a sky bridge to the International District Hotel. I explained a person called Eiko Egami had booked a room for me, and that I would be staying only a few days.

"Bit of a change of plan," said the concierge. Not what you want to hear after a long flight. "Some Australian killed her slave last night."

"Her slave?"

"Total riot."

The bags under my eyes tightened. "I don't think it's funny."

"No, a *literal* riot. We had to call the police." She saw something on her computer. "You're Nakadai, aren't you?"

"Am I getting her room?"

"Of course not! We may be Uliana's playground but we've got a business to run! What I *meant* to tell you was Eiko Egami would be staying with you. She's already up there."

Was there to be an *immovable mover*? A change-making thing that did not change itself?

I blushed. "What do you mean...she's *staying* with me?"

"You know how Akira Kurosawa looked when they buried him?"

"...Yes? Dead?"

"Well, she looks like that. Egami just finished her latest book, I'll have you know, and International District Hotels are *just* the kind of refuge crazy authors like her require. Do you write?"

"I'm a linguist. I write academic books."

The concierge sighed and gave me my key. I caught the lift to the 30th floor and walked down the greenish hall. The walls reminded me of my trainers. I reached the door, dropped my suitcase and beeped the door open.

The flush was violent. Egami emerged from the bathroom, victorious. She did a double-take when she saw me. "Oh, it's you..." she said.

"What are you doing here?" I came inside, dropped my suitcase and awaited her answer. "You're Egami, aren't you?"

She kicked her feet up, then switched on the television. "I had to go through a thousand-page manuscript deleting commas. What have you done?"

"I read your story—"

"*Might as well jump out the window*...what story?"

"*Philosophy of Burden*. Quite brilliant."

"Trash. Vulgar trash. Just like my landlord, Mr. Fumiyaki." She hopped off the bed and screwed up her leather-wallet-like face. "I had an apartment in Bunkyō until yesterday afternoon. I had an academic community surrounding me. And when I faced eviction, did any of them jump to my defence? Did a *single* one offer me refuge?"

I nodded sadly. There had been no charitable *impulse* for Eiko Egami.

"We can only be bothered to have solidarity when there's a strike. What solidarity is there in peacetime? None whatsoever. The hypocrisy is stunning. Now I've learned today they're discontinuing Creative Writing at the Tokyo Media School. They've agreed with your university to give us jobs on *your* campus. Why the *hell* should I believe them?" She paused. "Wait a minute... we're speaking English. Why the *hell* are we speaking English?"

"The thought had occurred to me—"

"Don't get funny with me *warugaki*—I know your game. You want to get me drunk. You want to do terrible things to my body. You want to abuse me, don't you? I've got news for you, *warugaki*, you don't have a chance. Get over there!"

There was a chair in the corner. I sat on it.

She ducked under the bed for a moment. When she reappeared, she held a shoebox. I gripped my nose because the smell was terrible. "What is *that*?"

"Dogshit. Someone sent it."

"No! No!"

"What's the matter?" she goaded. "Don't like a little modesty?" She waved the fecal equal of the *index of forbidden books* under my nose. "What's wrong with poo?"

"Get away from me!" I ran away from her; I jolted here and there about the room. "You're mad! You're stark-raving mad!"

"I bet you're a *scab*. Do you even know what a union *is*? Come back here, *warugaki!*" She opened the box and ran her fingers through the brown substance. "Oh God, it's *awful*. Come and feel this..."

"I shall not! I must...I must go over my notes for my lecture."

"If you're hoping to get away with an *indirect suicide*, I won't let you!" She twitched the fecal matter between her fingers. "Oh, *God*..." Then she looked at me. "Don't do the thing Barthes did."

"The, what?"

"Talk about what goes into writing a novel when you've never written a novel. Then claim you're morally superior because writers deal in fabrication, and you don't because you're a critic who deals with facts—*If you do that, I'll kill you! I'll drop my manuscript on your fucking head*!"

The room was an *incense boat.* I caught my breath and asked, "What is it about?"

"Kurosawa. *That's* what it's about. You know he loved Lenin, and got angry when people complained about the Soviet Union? What a guy."

"*Imprimatur...*"

"Speak up. I don't like it when you're quiet."

"*Let it be printed.* It is what a bishop says when they approve religious work for publication."

"And you're saying that's why I wrote my thousand-page manuscript?"

"I suppose so."

"Nakadai," she said, putting down the box of poo, "I think you're *great...*"

We stayed up most of the night; she with her thousand-page manuscript and I with my lecture notes.

At sunrise, she took me to the Tokyo Media School lamenting the impending loss of the Creative Writing department as she stalked the unhappy, bustling halls.

"There's nothing humane about the *Humanities*," she said, opening the lecture room door.

"That depends on who wrote the literature on the courses."

The Yamazaki Lecture Theatre was filled to the brim with students. I could hear Anglo-Saxon, Japanese and French. Postgraduates on the front row buttered croissants in Tupperware. Undergraduates sipped inexpensive, frog-coloured wine purchased from the Student Union Shop. There were as many shaved heads and unshaven legs as there were unshaven heads and shaven legs. A student body free from *rational freedom*, I thought. Shackled to their feelings, their minds were unenlightened by plausible faiths. Could I say that *I* had rational, *psychological* freedom?

A great fear came over me. I was as nervous as Peter of Spain had been when he penned *Summulae Logicales*: an Aristotelian textbook of logic featuring forays into what Wittgenstein would have called *modern logic*. "Are they expecting a lecture in English?" I asked Egami.

"Everything's taught in English. And these *worms* lap it up."

"Right." No one could enter heaven who had not been reborn of water and the Holy Spirit. I had to bathe these students in *something*.

"I am going to start by invoking *Inspector Miller and the Elasmobranch Banker*. I think you all know the fate of the Creative Writing department here. As far as I can understand, the reason for this is that there aren't enough people enrolling for that degree. Thus, the board of this university has decided, in its infinite wisdom, to get rid of the degree altogether. I am a linguist and teach in the Department of English Language and Literature. There we have disagreements among the staff. Some linguists think we should not be associated—taught alongside—literature. And some lecturers in literature and creative writing think they should not be taught alongside linguistics."

Perhaps I would convince this audience to *renounce* Satan?

"This is just the beginning. One day there won't *be* Humanities. The study and appreciation of literature will disappear, and so will the study of language. Where does this leave us? The world becomes an inhuman, inhospitable place in my version." I removed my light-slate-grey-coloured jacket and then wiped my forehead with an orange napkin. "I don't have to tell you the world is a mess. Here we have the *Nippon Progressives* opening copper and zinc mines; they send the stuff to Chinese governorships in Western Africa. Meanwhile in England, the *Reactionaries* are in power; they have been for the past 10 years. They *just* sold off the last locally-owned energy company to the Japanese government. In North America the Atlantan Republic declared itself *bankrupt*—the companies there write every operating system for every smartphone and laptop between here and Timbuktu, but somehow, they have gone bankrupt. They are *broke*; their employees are *broke*; they can't afford to send their children to university because their own country outlawed inheritance on the basis that it was *unfair*. It is impossible to outlaw unfairness anywhere today, however. And the more we lurch toward controlling how much money people have, the less money there seems to be. And this is *why* we need novelists. They remind us how crazy we are. They also don't *make* any money so they can't be *in it* for the money. And as for the *Elasmobranch Banker*—the banker did it."

I was confident now. I could speak the truth. "For the past 26 years—although I was probably destined to help it destroy the world—I have been under the influence of—"

Suddenly an unseen huddle of students burst in shouting obscenities in French. They pushed away their fellow students, blew air horns and shot confetti cannons toward me. They all wore squid hats with googly eyes and shouted, *"Le calmar est reel!"* in *bad* French.

"I knew it!" shouted Egami from her seat. "You might as well do porn!"

Putting to one side if the Japanese adult entertainment industry would indeed be a lucrative place to work when these students graduated, I was busy pondering their words.

Le calmar est reel? So *what* if the squid was real? Of course, squids were real. Then I remembered a less-than-profound proposition from *Translations* I suddenly realized they had taken *literally* and not *philosophically*.

The squid—in its capacity as a thing—has a type of grammar (semantics, phonology). It exists and travels through the world as that thing, that is, a squid. But if a squid were not a squid—it would be something different (inconsistent, clashing). Its phonology would be different; the world would be different; the squid would not be real (factual, historical).

Egami jumped down and pushed squid-orientated students away from me. I had, by this time, pulled my jacket over my head. I was crying, or something like it.

"Get away from him!" Egami screamed. "If you had watched *Throne of Blood* before you came, your plan would have worked!"

There emerged a fight between pro-Nakadai students and anti-Nakadai students, with Egami in the middle.

"Maybe this is it, Nakadai?" she said to me as police filed in to break up the fight. "Tomorrow we'll be building houses from newspapers, and children will be pickled and eaten. I won't have to write because I'll be spending my time foraging for food!"

No such thing happened. The squid-orientated students, led by undergraduate Saburo Yager, were dragged into the courtyard by police.

They were beaten, thrown into a police van and taken to the nearest police station, which, as any Japanese will tell you, is *not* a place you want to visit.

We stood back up. I blew out my cheeks. "Do you know anything about Teilhardism?"

"The Jesuit?"

"He said the universe was subject to *four* stages. It seems we are stuck on the third stage: the *noo-genesis*, where living things become *rational* beings."

"I think the police acted rationally. If you saw *Ran* you would understand."

"*King Lear* is hardly a good advertisement for the running of the state," I said.

Egami stared at me. "Let's get lunch."

We walked out of the lecture room, down the corridor and into the staff room. Daichi Murakami, who specialized in literature written in the *Abun* language, was sitting alone eating what appeared to be some twigs. He looked at Egami for a split second, then went back to his twigs.

Egami cut her eyes. "*Ohayō.*"

"*Konnichiwa,*" he replied suspiciously.

She opened a fridge, took out two Tupperwares and gave me one. We sat at a separate table, eating our soy-soaked rice. "Murakami." The man said nothing. "Murakami, I want to talk to you."

He put down his chopsticks. "What is it?"

"A little *tori* told me you're happy to see Creative Writing go. Just seems a bit hypocritical."

He reddened. "Who told you that?"

"Nakadai thinks you're stupid too."

He looked at me. "Just to confirm," I said, "I don't even know you."

"You hear that, Murakami?" Egami was smiling. "He doesn't even know you! Imagine that: your work is so un-cool that Nakadai doesn't even know you."

Daichi stood up. He had had quite enough. "I will be seeing you in the departmental this afternoon. Until then—*evil cause, evil effect.*" He picked up his things and left.

"*Metempsychosis,*" she declared. "The transmigration of the soul from one body to another. I think you can appreciate that."

"What do you mean?"

"Murakami is Saburo Yager's cousin. Twice-removed, but the resemblance is palpable."

"He is the one who organized the protest?" I asked.

"Saburo's name means the *third son*. There's some sexual deviancy going on. He doesn't know anything about Kuroswa or Lenin; nor does he understand fascism. He *thinks* he understands feminism but he doesn't."

"What are we on *now*?"

"Eighth Wave—get with it, Nakadai." She coughed. "There are two main philosophers Saburo Yager should have started with. The first one, Marion Shelton, thinks men shouldn't be allowed to make ethical decisions about lives outside their own because they don't have reproductive organs. The second one, Queen Uliana of Algeria, adopts what Bishop Berkeley thought about everything and applies it to men. She argues men are *merely concepts*, and because they're only concepts, they don't exist so you can treat them however you want. As you can imagine she gets interviewed more—despite her being a *man*, but we don't talk about that."

"That was good rice," I said.

"It's not mine..."

I woefully misplaced the remainder of that particular fictionalization, even if what appeared gave a good indication of Nakadai's unwieldy return to Japan. Now, as for the remainder of his *trip*, I can but briefly, describe how it ended.

In amanner akin to Nam June Paik's destructive, multimedia performances, Egami battered Nakadai awake with her thousand-page manuscript and forced him out of the hotel room. He regrettably left Egami to settle the bill and crossed the sky bridge into the airport where he purchased a *new* return ticket. Exhausted as though he had played a lengthy solo in a *chamber symphony*, he slept on a bench in the departure lounge and awoke to find his luggage had been stolen. He subsequently became the prime suspect in a Maigret-like investigation that lasted some 2 hours. In the nick of time, the luggage was discovered in a Burger King kitchen where it was revealed the kitchen porter had stolen the luggage because he thought it looked nice. The departure lounge speakers started playing Ryuichi Sakamoto's *Merry Christmas, Mr. Lawrence* theme when Nakadai sprinted for the departure gate which, as always, was several miles from the departure lounge. He stepped safely onto the plane and found his seat where he slept for 12 miserable hours thereafter. When he awoke the old woman next to him smiled and whispered, "Leaving again, are we?" in broken Japanese. He had no idea who, or what, she was.

Given the pedigree of the Tokyo Media School where Nakadai had given his lecture and the undoubted appreciation for his work under the malevolent wardship of Professor Mutton who, somewhat oafishly, publicly declared his ex-student to be the smartest man in the world, the 49-year-old Nakadai stood a good chance if he were to put himself forward for the chair of Professor of Neo-Linguistics which the apparently-ageless Mutton intended to relinquish.

The old chair had nominated the new chair in private, of course, and explained that Nakadai hadn't the choice to refuse it as it would anger his master and bring down the whole roof onto their heads. In what appeared to be a conditional excellence on par with Joan Cross founding the National School of Opera in 1948, Nakadai opted to *accept* Mutton's perilous private offer. Regardless, the election process still went ahead without rigging and Professor Mutton urged Nakadai to keep his mouth shut.

Around the same time, Goro Saito revealed to Nakadai that he was becoming a Senior Lecturer in Language, Cognition & Neuroscience. Preoccupied with his potential, reluctant professorship, Nakadai merely nodded. Just this time, it seemed, his everlasting cognitive bondage won over his predilection to obstinate jealousy.

Nakadai duly applied for the post of Professor of Philosophy and submitted a part of his book, *Translations*, in support. The other two candidates were Dr. Omar Braddock and Dr. Zeta Palazzo. Despite Professor Mutton's séance-like activities which guided the election process, Nakadai was positive that the chair would go to Palazzo. She was rightly revered and admired by the department as well as being in the pocket of Professor Duni Mwangangi—a man who could stand neither Nakadai nor his bizarre, antagonistic work.

But it's sheer poppycock to argue there was even the remotest possibility that Nakadai would *not* be made the new Professor of Neo-Linguistics. He was, as *Translations* had demonstrated, the foremost linguistic genius of his time and was dedicated to an extent that it made Palazzo and Braddock look like obstinate freeloaders. In other words, to *refuse* the chair to Nakadai would have been the equivalent of refusing Mendelssohn the right to study under Zelter in Berlin; refusing Seiji Ozawa the tutorship of Karajan; or, indeed, making it somehow impossible for Eminem to have met Dr. Dre. Thus, even if there were those such as Mwangangi who thought little of Nakadai's linguistic contributions, they still would have been unbalanced to comment that Nakadai was not qualified for the chair of Professor of Neo-Linguistics.

Professor Mutton took Nakadai aside when the verdict was announced. "In religion as you well know," he explained, "it does not matter if the words used are true or false. It follows, then, that your servitude is right in every light. And if you carry on serving you shall become a God!"

This was a promise, notwithstanding, that would be cut short in the same way that Schumann's *Abegg Variations* peter out in their final movements. It would be met with a slurry of resistance that neither Professor Mutton nor the Reperio Society; nor even the infinite fail-safe faculties of Nakadai could have predicted.

The University, Work & College Union would, once again, toss their spanner into the warped machines of high finance and slow the deceitful revolutions of numerous cogs therein...

> To exhaustively comprehend the Higher Education Strike we must turn, in the course of our narrative, to a woman who was the *hurdy-gurdy* to Nakadai's *guitar*. Kotori Chiba, that brave maternal aunt who had taken Nakadai in after his mother and father had perished, had been missing her nephew for some time. He had succumbed to the influence of Professor Mutton and the Great Word—as well as the prospect of producing a PhD of merit—and seldom communicated with Ms. Chiba. Their sometimes-absurd correspondence bore a great tonal

likeness to Falla's opera, *Master Peter's Puppet Show*, based upon *Don Quixote*'s 26th chapter and about *half* as funny...

Having left her Asian Supermarket in a safe pair of Malaysian hands, however, the 89-year-old Ms. Chiba was in no position to relax her familial ties. Indeed, in one's retirement, it becomes easy to forget about discipline, rigour and the forged happiness of uneasy emotional toil, so beautifully illustrated by Henry Purcell's unfinished *Indian Queen*. Thus Ms. Chiba was determined that she would *not* go the way of so many retirees, and would instead spend a great many hours with her good friend, Ms. Doris Dingle—the infamous matriarch of the Dingletones—and convulse with laughter, tell gratuitous stories, reflect upon past and future success, wiling the time away with something approaching total refinement or nirvana. *These would be the happiest of times*, Ms. Chiba was determined to prove to herself, especially in the presence of Ms. Dingle who, with her inane head of fiery red hair and pear-like disposition, forever proved to be the finest of listeners and the warmest of heart. And so once again I must retire the reins momentarily to Nakadai himself who, with his own embellished record, should illustrate an accurate picture of the Higher Education Strike and the part his aunt, Ms. Chiba, played in it. The following was described to me by my maternal aunt, Ms. Chiba, at her residence in Twickley, after I had received a few stitches on my forehead at the behest of Dr. Vanya Dubey:

It had already been an impulsive day of chores when Ms. Chiba, resident of No. 15 Marlowe Road, was called upon by that infamous matriarch of the Dingletone family, Ms. Doris Dingletone, known affectionately always as Ms. Doris *Dingle*—for, it was quicker to pronounce and more redolent of the jolly experiential frame she possessed—to attend high tea that sunny winter morning.

Ms. Chiba, determined as she was to pursue her attainment of total refinement through her splendid jaunts with Ms. Dingle, accepted in a heartbeat and set to shutting the curtains, blowing out the candles—as she preferred candlelight to the luminous stuff emitted from lightbulbs—dressing in her jeans, black top and tiny colourful scarf, then locked up her abode and set off down Marlowe Road—which itself was a steep hill lined with a comprehensive school and tall trees—into the city centre of Twickley, which was as busy as a frog pond that day.

In the green-attired and furniture-laden Queen Square Tea Room, opposite the Dingletone family home—the imposingly large and posh No. 2 Queen Square—our two ladies greeted each other with pecks on the cheek, were seated and ordered bancha tea. With this, the dispatched personal host prepared a portable charcoal fire at their table, scooped quantities of water with a bamboo dipper into a stout kettle and placed the kettle onto the glowing embers. As the water began to bubble, the host returned with a plate of unpretentious cakes, a tea bowl from which their tea would be served, and a larger bowl for the melancholy leafings of the tea.

Ms. Dingle initiated polite conversation as the tea was prepared: "Ah, we are both single mothers in our ways, aren't we Kotori?"

Ms. Chiba agreed, stating that it must be difficult with her husband having died only recently and with all of her children at boarding school.

"Yes, we all have our crosses to bear, don't we?" Ms. Dingle replied. "And speaking of crosses—if you excuse the heretic connection—how is your *son* doing; that Nakadai of yours?"

"Well, he was never my son, you see. I never thought of Nakadai as a son, more as a—to use the *heretical connection*, as you say—he was more of a lamb. You should always want to take care of lambs, I think."

"This is true, very true—" Such were the poetic and commonplace topics of high tea. "But lambs, too, must grow and they get bigger and bigger. Thank you—" Their host poured their tea, bowed smiling and retired to another table on the other side of the room. "Mmm, lovely—but yes, Nakadai is very old now—"

"Very old? I am very old! Not him, compared to me, he might as well be at school."

"In many ways, he never left school, wouldn't you agree?"

"Yes, yes, I would agree—well put, Ms. Dingle—" I don't believe my aunt knew the woman's Christian name. "But I haven't seen him in the longest time, you know; he stays up there, at his school, the university, doing God knows what—Ugh! It infuriates me!"

"I can see, I can see—but why don't you contact him, tell him to pay attention to his poor aunt." Ms. Chiba resented being called the "poor aunt" greatly. "Why, it must have been some time since you saw him last?"

"I believe the last time I saw Nakadai was 3 of your Anglo-Saxon Christmases ago."

"What! That is *most* unsatisfactory! And this Nakadai has no one else with whom to spend his time?" Ms. Dingle enquired in a state of shock unwitnessed so far in the Queen Square Tea Room.

"No, I don't think so—unless he goes back to that damned monastery, I mean "abbey", sorry—I am worried, as you can see."

"There's no wonder why you're so worried! Such a thing would never happen to the Dingletones," she added not altogether helpfully. "Not with myself as the matriarch; that would never happen—never! No, I think it's a sin that he hasn't seen you in 3 years."

But the 89-year-old Ms. Chiba and the 87-year-old Ms. Dingle were in no position, arguably, to make demands upon anyone, for is it not true that the world has left behind such people in the later stages of aging? And must we, the young, habitually heed the doddery contrivances of antiquity's custodians? These are questions, stark queries, that not even the pampered and proud Ms. Dingle could have begun to articulate answers for. As for Ms. Chiba, she was more resigned than her accomplice, thinking herself the last of her race as none but herself had survived the age-related dilapidation of her family. Now she was alone.

"Which is why my nephew is a kind of relic in his own right," Ms. Chiba went on to her progressively angrier accomplice. "He, too, is the "last of his race", if you understand my meaning."

And she began to weep, a most unusual occurrence for any participant of high tea.

"There, there," Ms. Dingle, with great affection, patted the wrinkly upper side of Ms. Chiba's manly paw. "Don't get upset, my dear. I am here, aren't I? And there should never be any reason to be lonely and disaffected with me, my dear. What is that idiom of yours you always repeat to me? *Nanakorobi yaoki.* "Fall seven times and stand up eight." And you, with your business record, have surely stood up eight times by now?"

"Yes, I suppose I have, but at the cost of seven droppings!"

"That is everyone's story, surely? Tell you what: where do you stand on the Higher Education Strike?"

"The *what*?"

"The Higher Education Strike—everyone's talking about it. It's brought the country to a standstill."

"Nakadai will know something about that!" Ms. Chiba ventured bravely, happily.

"Should you like me to explain the particulars, causes, as far as I know?" asked Ms. Dingle.

"Why, of course! If it means I'll get closer to my nephew." And such mild philosophical discussions, carried out perpetually in a state of universal agreement, are also the lot of high tea, especially when older reflective ladies are involved. "Alright then, go on—explain it to me!"

"Right, you've put me on the spot, Kotori! Ha-ha! Let's see—well, it's always got something to do with money, hasn't it? From what I gather, Kotori, all the universities in the country, except those which operate as independents, are run by a thing called the Reperio Society."

"I see," said Ms. Chiba, "and who are the Reperio Society?"

"They're a subsidiary of the Society of Jesus, the Jesuits, who were positively smashing with their emphasis on literacy, et cetera. They even made it to Japan, didn't they? But you doubtless know more about this than I do, ah yes, certainly you do, you must—judging by your silence you don't—oh well! Let me continue then on this little tract of mine. Oh, it *is* excellent tea here, isn't it? So, Francis Xavier and Ignatius of Loyola started the Jesuits and I'm sure you know this since it's a part of your country's strange history," she said strange as though it had caused her an ulcer. "So, basically, my dear, Rome seems to have taken an interest in Anglo-Saxon higher education over 200 years ago, so they founded the Reperio Society and gradually seeped into the running of all these research institutions."

"That sounds ridiculously barmy," said Ms. Chiba suddenly. "Why, you expect me to *believe* that some Roman organization squirreled its way into running these Anglo-Saxon universities? Maybe they put something in our tea and plan to surprise us with something!"

"Oh, really! Don't be so crude—you Japanese are always so crude!" Ms. Dingle, the infamous Ms. Dingle, began to seem distressed at Ms. Chiba's presence alone. "The point anyway is that there's a thing called an Exalted President in the Reperio Society who runs it, you see, and this person—who is a woman I might add—decided to make some alterations to the Reperio Welfare Scheme."

"Nakadai's money!"

"Yes, Nakadai's money, my dear; only from teaching, I assume—unless he squeezed a few private pounds in there, eh, Kotori?"

"I wouldn't lend Nakadai money in a million years! He wouldn't know what to do with it anyway. He'd probably just buy a few more beach chairs and slim detective novels. Or that Perfect Word he goes on about. You know he has no clue how to enjoy himself."

"Verily," Ms. Dingle remarked, "but in all fairness to yourself it is just a quarterly pension scheme, my dear. But the Exalted President—who's a woman, yes!

a woman—decided to raise the contribution from 9% to 20%, which I think is a very good thing to do."

"Well, that sounds like theft to me," said Ms. Chiba wisely. "Daylight robbery, that sounds like to me—say, they didn't connect all this money, the pool of contributions, to the stock market by any chance, did they?"

"Funnily enough that too is a point of contention amongst the academics, or whatever they call themselves. *Readers in X*. But yes, so what happened was the University, Work & College Union decided to call a strike and it's still going on today!"

"Where is it, I mean—where does it take place?"

"At the university of course! They've withdrawn teaching, all of it. Positively barmy, yes, you spoke of "barmy" things earlier, didn't you?"

"I did, I did—but if I had any idea Nakadai was part of this—no, it's not very good at all—how do they get away with it, that is, the withdrawal of teaching services?"

"Well, they just do it, don't they?"

"But do they get paid?" asked Ms. Chiba.

"Certainly not! The university's refusing to pay them and these talks are ongoing, negotiations they call them—if they were to keep on teaching, there would be little to bargain with, would there? Meaning the teaching staff, lecturers and professors, have to withhold something to put pressure on the university. Now that I think about it, it makes rather a lot of sense to me. Yes, and what about those who love teaching, eh? What becomes of them?"

"I don't suppose you *have* to go on strike," said Ms. Chiba.

"No, quite right, Kotori, you don't have to go on strike. I say—is Nakadai a member of a union?"

"I haven't a clue—I'm certainly not and never have been, as I'm antagonistic towards any organization who claims to be the emotional and rights-orientated voice of a group of human beings. I don't see how anybody could get on board with that."

"Perhaps, when you are overworked and underpaid, one might begin to think about subscribing to such a movement?"

"Maybe," Ms. Chiba caught a glimpse of another customer's breath gliding like a cloud across the cool window. "But the proclivity for misinformation is much too high for my liking and probably Nakadai's too—oh, I do wish we could see him! And as another refutation, so to speak, regardless of how good the intentions of the union are, I have a right to think I'm correct, even if I'm wrong. And so, I have a right *not* to strike, and for that decision to be respected. So, any organization who doesn't want me exercising that right is a dangerous one."

Ms. Dingle, having finished her tea, dumped the leafy fragrant remains into the larger bowl provided. "It's a good thing we agree on so many things—I can't get behind anything you're saying. You've got to think about the greater good, my dear. Because if we don't fight together, then there's no hope of anything ever getting fixed."

"Nothing ever *does* get fixed, Ms. Dingle." She thought deeply about what Ms. Dingle's real name might be and was left none the wiser. 'should we go find Nakadai?"

"YES!" Ms. Dingle exclaimed, causing several customers to spill their tea out of sheer fright. "Yes, I think that is a perfectly *splendid* idea! Two old biddies! Off we go!"

With a rapidity that frightened even the ancient finely-toned hosts of the Queen Square Tea Room, Ms. Chiba and Ms. Dingle exited the premises, hailed a cab—as both ladies were of the opinion that only they would spend the capital they'd accumulated—and spied the passing perpendicular housing blocks, beautiful antiquated terraced housing, yellowish buses filled with university students and infrequent grumpy academics, wide frozen fields beset by swollen sheep and finally the grand super-signed entrance to the University of Twickley, which was rammed with academics from both the regular university and the medical school, as well as what appeared to be undergraduate students. "Students stand with seminar leaders?" Ms. Chiba read one of the placards held aloft. "I certainly don't agree with that."

"Nor do I, my dear, they're going to get hurt standing out there." Ms. Dingle tapped the glass partition causing the taxi driver to brake abruptly. The wealthy widow paid the fee, took her accomplice by the hand and stepped into the bright chilly January air. "Now, *this* is what I call theatre!"

"I don't know, Ms. Dingle—they look—violent."

"Nakadai!" Ms. Dingle began to vaguely shout at the crowd, as though I would appear like a mushroom amongst the bark. "Nakadai! Where are you!"

"Don't do that! Don't call his name!"

"Why not, pray?" Ms. Dingle watched a group of students with shaven heads waving huge signs shouting "Free Nakadai!".

She said to her accomplice: "Hold on a moment—look at that, there! Look at those signs. They say Free Nakadai! What on Earth for, I wonder?"

"Yes, my goodness, this is most peculiar, which is in fitting with this "peculiar" nephew of mine; shall we go ask them what it's all about?"

And Ms. Chiba and Ms. Dingle, their expensive clothing drawing the glances of some of the poorer attendees at the picket line, trotted up to the pugnacious pack of pitiless students, their tumultuous screechy voices forming far more vapours than would otherwise have occurred.

"Look at these old bags, look at them!" said one student wearing a Nakadai tee shirt. "What do you want? Get out of here! You don't belong here; this isn't your fight!" Which immediately confused the old biddies as surely the strike was a matter for the employees to discuss; and students were not, despite their fees and occasional paid work, employees of the university, beholden to it in any way.

"Nakadai is my nephew!" Ms. Chiba shouted back. "How dare you talk to me like that!"

"What—you're his—you're what?"

"I'm Nakadai's auntie, I'll have you know. Now, tell me, as his name is a matter of intellectual property—namely, my intellectual historical familial property—why do you have his name up in the air like that? It's most annoying!"

The voice of the elderly Japanese woman had drawn other students around the two old biddies and Ms. Dingle began to suspect their intentions were not entirely peaceful. "Steady on, Kotori," she whispered to her now red-faced accomplice. "You're aggravating them—"

"Basically," proclaimed another student sheepishly, "we think Nakadai's being mistreated—our lecturer, Nakadai, the Professor of Neo-Linguistics—and you say you're his auntie, which is great and all, but that doesn't concern us because we're anti-family, more or less. And believe that bloodlines are a social construct created by the patriarchy to enforce ignoble securities."

"Let me make sense of this drivel," Ms. Chiba remarked. "You don't think families exist—but I'll have you know that there's a lot more to families than blood! Families, groups in which everyone is related are not necessarily a matter of biological connection—what am I getting at here, Ms. Dingle? Why it's very simple and fundamental, it's a simple fundamental point: if you don't believe in families, then you can't possibly believe in love, either! Not in any kind of long-lasting functional love, certainly—you mean to tell me you don't think families exist, beyond those constructs you mentioned, of course?"

"No, we do not." All the Free Nakadai! signs lowered slightly, like a balloon being emptied slowly of its air. "More importantly, though, Professor Mutton—*emeritus* he may be—is a dangerous influence upon this place and he needs to go! Look, look, everyone, look! There he goes!"

Professor Mutton's car drove through the picket. Eggs and tomatoes were thrown at it.

"I don't believe it!" said another student. "He's crossed the picket line! The yucky fetid tosser! I can't imagine anyone loves him!"

"I suspect Nakadai's crossed the picket line as well," thought Ms. Chiba, but would never in a million years say that because despite Ms. Dingle's sporadic anti-Japanese sentiment, she liked the old widow for her jolly outlook and no-nonsense inclinations and would never say anything that would put the capital old newt in danger.

And so, a better part of the day went by, the students explaining their relationships with me, chanting mystic rhythmic songs in an attempt to levitate the university, laughing and telling jokes with Ms. Chiba, criticizing the infamous Ms. Dingle at almost every opportunity and shooting her untrustworthy glances, informing Ms. Chiba—whom they were now referring to as Auntie Chiba—that she had passed their tests, even though she didn't really agree with some of the ludicrous out-of-touch views they had and believed genuinely that the later impending ramifications of these radical and irresponsible beliefs would indeed be as odious, unholy and crooked as the now-retired Professor Mutton they were so determined to irrevocably smear. But they were young and had to be forgiven. "It's essential that we do that," Ms. Chiba nobly thought...

Thus, the adventures of Ms. Chiba and Doris Dingle, the infamous matriarch of the Dingletones, came to a close when Ms. Dingle desired to return home and catch the first episode of the new *Inspector Miller* series on ITV3, so she ushered the now revered and continually hooted-at Ms. Chiba into yet another taxi, after which the thenceforward depressed vehicle pooted into the distance, a duo of disputing exhilarated silhouettes dancing in the back window cut by the dying light of that lugubrious January day...

Nakadai's account above smacks of Warlock's *Capriol* and, therefore, of twisted reproductions of Renaissance dancing. Regardless, Nakadai had crossed the picket line and was a scab forever sullied in the jaded eyes of his departmental colleagues. The strike affected two million students overall and led to the formation of a militant advocacy group known officially as Verified University Learning Vestibule for Advancement and unofficially as VULVA. Like Rudolf Kempe and his oboe, they broke into the accounting offices of the university, demanded their fees be refunded and threatened to kill staff. They were forced out by an accountant who, like the multi-talented oboist Rudolf Kempe, furtively carried his own Glock. This sticky deed saw VULVA target academics, one of whom was a lecturer in Chemistry & Forensic Science called Allesandro Dekker. Having made eye contact with a woman for longer than two seconds, he was sentenced to death via *galliard* and "danced upon till he did gasp for breath and dyed".

This violent turn of events escalated the strike to an all-out war in which the students—whose views were not endorsed by the strike which had nothing to do with them anyway—and the Upper Loxhall Constabulary were the key players. Thus, on the same day Ms. Chiba secured her rhetorical victory with the students, there came a crushing physical defeat with Nakadai who, having escaped the fortified library, found himself stuck in the university square. On one side the riot police were shooting real bullets from atop a blockade, while on the other VULVA members burnt books and sang strange quarrelsome motets:

> There were two things the Japanese had trouble understanding when Francis Xavier first visited Japan. They could not understand how a God who had created everything, including evil, could possibly be *good*. Nor were they comfortable with their

ancestors suffering eternity in hell. When I left the library that day, I found myself asking the very same questions—I seemed to access *race memory* when that bunch of police officers started making fun of me. They wore dense armour and carried AR-15s. They had been called in to deal with strikers and anti-strikers, but now they were faced with someone who wanted nothing to do with either group. They asked me strange questions: Was this my *normal* accent? When did I *arrive* in the country? How *long* had I been here? I realized they were making fun of me when someone asked me about Godzilla. I said I did not know anything about Godzilla; I had not seen him in years. They did *not* like my reply. They seemed to cover me; hands hovered over holsters. "I bet you don't have a clue about war," someone said; and I replied, "I will have you know I served in Japan's Self-Defence Force—so don't lecture *me* about war." Suddenly their superior marched through them. He had green eyes and was cultured. He took off his helmet, and said, 'thank you, ladies and gentlemen. And what do we have here? *You* wouldn't know public service if it hit you in the face—" He punched my left cheek, and down I went. The ground gave me those stitches I had later. I listened to their laughter and grew angrier by the minute. I could not think of anything to say, however. I was *down* there, and they were *up* there. Gradually sinister tones re-entered the group. Their leader, DCI Lumb, wrapped tape over my mouth. He dragged me up scaffolding overlooking the university square and dangled me to the anti-strikers like a frightened hunk of meat. How *could* God have created people like this? How could God be *good* when injurious creations like this one marshalled control and got what they wanted through brute force? The man dangling me had no fear of hell; he had concluded, in his own brutal time, that hell did not exist. Then his inferiors started firing into the crowd. They hit some students; others they wounded. There was smoke and flame and shouting. (Either God willed this or we were *all* going to hell, I thought.) I was fuming when they lowered me down the scaffolding. I breathed heavily and angrily; I could have done anything I wanted. Their superior continued prodding me, calling me names and slapping me about the head. Then something in me—a momentary loss of faith—stretched the existential elastic *too* far. I jabbed my fingers in DCI Lumb's right eye and he screamed like a child. He lunged backwards in pain, then forward, his colleagues aiming to shoot. "Stop! Leave him!" He waved his colleagues away. He spied me with the remaining eye, and said, "You can go. You go back to wherever you came from. You remember something, though—I'll be coming to get you!" I freed my mouth, grabbed my rucksack and ran as quickly as possible. I cut corners and dodged doors. Finally, I reached Arkham Main and went to my office. I slept

> there that night and by the morning I had found my faith. I remembered Professor Mutton, however, and knew it would be tested...

In March the Higher Education Strike, much like Donizetti's opera of Anne Boleyn's life, reached an unpunctual favourable finale. After a series of protracted negotiations, the Reperio Society and the University, Work & College Union agreed that employee contributions would be raised over a period of 8 years. It was also agreed that university employees would be given a Twickley Bundle of only partial strike pay. And it was around the same time that, in light of the Free Nakadai! placards, Nakadai was given a verbal whipping in Mutton's office.

Verily, Nakadai would never have expected that one day he'd have become so influential that his actions and relationships would be discussed on as high a level as talks between the union and the Reperio Society. But this was not a good thing. Because it demonstrated the university's lack of understanding about Nakadai's relationship with Professor Mutton and the Great Word, as it proved how the latter two egregious forces had been doing their utmost to keep their secrets from the world of mankind. There was no hope for Nakadai and the next 6 years would prove to be the hardest and most fatiguing years of his life...

13

MYSELF—AGAINST TRAINING —CAPTAIN KHUHRO—THREE MODULES OF DEATH

With our narrative at peak velocity, it becomes necessary to say how I met the peculiar Nakadai. He was already halfway through his erstwhile career as a Benedictine monk when I was christened Nicola Hillam-Joiner in ——. My mother was a musicologist and my father was an archaeologist; since neither career pays very well I grew up rather modestly and attended St. John's College in the busy college-town of Marlborough. I grew up listening to the music of Pietro Aaron and the *zarzuelas* of Francisco Barbieri; the clarinets of Henrik Crusell and the orchestrations of Paul Dukas *among others*. (I learnt nothing of health inspection or medicine because my father was irritatingly well-travelled and seemed to be going everywhere but home constantly.) I was thoroughly middle-of-the-road academically and scored B's and C's.

I became interested in language when, after *reading* the secular songs of Jacopo de Bologna, I considered what Claude

Shannon would have referred to as the fundamental problem facing communication, *that is*, how the receiver is able to *identify* the kind of information—generated by the *source*—which has travelled along the *channel*. The interplay of channel, transference and information mesmerized me and I decided to go to university to further its potential in my mind.

I was accepted by Brexton University during clearing which demonstrated that the philosophy of universities was not to assist in the formation of knowledge but to make money. I studied linguistics there and was accepted for an MA in Applied Linguistics & Communication. It was around this time that Brexton University attempted to define and rail against certain groups' innate privileges. When I re-registered for my MA I was asked to fill out a questionnaire which constituted a complete breakdown of my psychology, heritage and income. It was the one time I disliked being the daughter of my mother; during our welcome week, I was sent along with the other creatives to the most extensive of Brexton University's new thought-crime seminars. These were seminars in which students, given their questionnaire answers, were lectured on their innate privileges and how injurious they were to less corrupted students.

I was singled out by Rowena Tosh, our seminar leader, and hounded for my innate creative tendencies. I should not mix with non-creative students on accounting and finance courses, she argued, because I was psychologically incapable of understanding them and posed a series of psychological threats; not because of anything I had said or *would* say, but because of my innate psychological heritage and whatever income I experienced, therefore.

"Excuse me—" I looked around the other students. "Is anyone else bothered by this?"

"I'm thankful you interrupted me, Nicola," Rowena said, then addressed the others. 'this is what we call a *resentment rush*, which has far too many syllables; but we are working with our directors to realize—that means, *create*—a better term for this sort of behaviour."

"Why can't Michelle do that?" I pointed to the girl next to me. "Why can't she do that?"

"Nicola," Rowena smiled, "we are 5 hours in; we have *two* more to go. Now, could you just save your questions till the end?"

"No, I can't, because I'm done," I said. "You've been telling us that we're evil when we haven't done anything."

"That's what *you* think—"

"But you don't know us, Rowena! You don't know any of us! My mum is Pakistani and my dad's English; Michelle's are Swedish; Mike was born in Iran and raised in Norway and now lives in London. Do you know how I know that? Because I spoke to them while we were waiting for this seminar—which you were *late* for! You were late for your *own* seminar! You have no values, no beliefs—all you do is peddle some weird religion to people you can't even be bothered to understand!"

"This here," Rowena said, "is a serious *resentment rush*. If we don't engage her, class, then we should be alright."

Michelle raised her hand. "I'm confused."

"Yes, Michelle?"

"I did the questionnaire and I got the "creative" designation and sent it here—but I'm doing accounting and finance. So—why is that?"

Rowena's voice cracked. "These are...irregularities that get ironed out as the process continues."

"What does that mean?" I asked.

"You need to listen, Nicola; if you don't listen you will be liable for *expulsion*."

The students gasped. I scrutinized Rowena and said, "If I don't pass this course—I get expelled?"

"That's correct."

"Goodness," I said. "We haven't started our coursework and already we're cynical. That's what you want; you *want* us to be cynical. You don't want us to be *sceptical*. Do you agree?"

Rowena was sincere in her cardigan: "Scepticism, without a doubt, is the *most* creative quality. It's no good, Nicola—we don't want that here."

I was shaking. "You want us to condemn prior to investigation. That's what you want. I'm going to go a step further—I don't think anyone who believes in courses like this one can know what they want. If you practice condemnation prior to investigation then you will *never* in a million years know what satisfies you. You are going to live in a permanent state of dissatisfaction and foist that unhappiness on other people in the same way that you have done today. None of us, I'm sure, are satisfied with your dissatisfaction. I can only say that I feel pity for you. It's sad that you don't believe in anything; that you have no values. You have no values because you condemn potential lessons; and you don't believe in anything because you're without education, therefore, and cannot believe in yourself. You feel stupid—I can't blame you. You have lost faith in yourself; you hate yourself and the people who *taught* you, however ironically, to hate yourself are going to hell. They are probably already there. Their hell is the reality they've carved out for themselves—not, as Sartre would like us to believe, *other people*. Other people didn't raise me—my parents did. Other people didn't make me go to St. John's in Marlborough—that's all that was available to me at the time. If I were to condemn the time in which I was born, how arrogant would that be? That would place me up there with people like Lenin who viewed people as chemical compounds to be mixed and experimented with—as opposed to human beings who needed to be governed, or loved. We like to think students are fully-formed by the time they get to university, but they're not. They are children—I am a child; and who are you to condemn a child to die before they have even lived? If I were to die tomorrow, I would be miffed! I would be so angry! I'd be furious because I would know that instead of going out and buggering things up—which is the only way to learn anything—I sat for 7 hours listening to some emotional cripple explain why I shouldn't be allowed to grow... and how *dare* you call me resentful; wouldn't *you* be resentful if someone *bullied* you?"

The following year Brexton University discarded these thought-crime seminars in the same way that Elizabeth Maconchy, following the tutorship of Vaughn Williams, abandoned serial procedure and embraced chromatic freedom. Moreover, it was around this time that I thought about doing a PhD. The very *thought* of this, however, seemed to irritate my tutor, Dr. Phillipa Foster, who immediately ranted about how difficult it would be. This would be no *carol*, she argued, but a mighty, ever-changing composition that would make Scarlatti's

Cat's Fugue appear to be the most uncomplicated music ever composed. Foster described how endlessly competitive and quite awful it would be and that I should take a year off to think about it more seriously. This irritated me in turn and seemed ludicrous to think I hadn't thought seriously about engaging in doctoral studies; no more preposterous than the composer Paul Creston not thinking seriously about the importance of Gregorian chants and their influence on his music. Indeed, the fact that I was even *enquiring* about doctoral studies should have been tantamount to my having seriously thought about such a dangerous commitment.

I was bloody-minded and sought out a PhD tutor. After researching various individuals, I settled on Hiroshi Nakadai at the University of Twickley. I had heard a few stories about the man; I was fascinated by him and sent off the obligatory awkward email.

"He doesn't take many on, you know," Foster warned me. "I doubt very much that he'll take you on and that doesn't reflect on your talents; rather, it reflects on the fact that he's a difficult man! Yes! He is a *very* annoying and elusive man!"

(I later learned that she had been trying for years to organize a visiting lecture from Nakadai. And that Nakadai had never had the good fortune to retrieve her emails from his *junk-mail* folder.)

Thankfully, after about a week of waiting, he replied to *me* and agreed to supervise my PhD in Theoretical & Applied Linguistics. I was Elizabeth Maconchy and he, in the guise of Vaughn Williams, had decided to educate me in the sonic method of music. He added that he was extremely busy, notwithstanding, and expected me to do the heavy lifting myself. The prospect of working with *the* Hiroshi Nakadai suddenly seemed so real and exciting, however, and I agreed to his terms. I subsequently moved to Twickley with a mind to starting my doctorate in September.

It is very easy to think that your work is less important than your tutor's when your scholastic efforts are pitted against theirs. What I found encouraging about Nakadai was his own belief that he was still a student and therefore would demand as much limited respect as I gave him. Thus, I will not describe my PhD thesis in detail, but instead, include one of my fictionalizations.

What follows, dear reader, is something that happened early on in my relationship with Nakadai. It demonstrated that trouble seemed to follow Nakadai wherever he went. And I hope that you will forgive the occasional, fabricated tableau contained within this short story.

> A rainy day on campus, a ding of an email, then this: *What is this private hell I'm in? I met you a long time ago, Nakadai, but I remember you. We've got an understanding of madness, the two of us, but if you couple the insides, the stinking thinking, there's four of us. There's a climber. There's a climber and he's climbing and he falls. He doesn't fall to his death, if you get what I'm saying; what I mean is he's falling and falling, for so long he doesn't know which way is up. He may be falling up. You're reading this, I can tell you understand, I can feel it ripping through. My problem is I don't know which direction my madness is going. There's an old word, madness (mania, hysteria, frenzy).*

I'm here and there, I say to myself, "God help me..." But God only helps me when I'm angry. Do you understand? I know you understand, I've established that. But if God only helps me when I'm angry, doesn't that set me up for failure? A truly Christian failure? I mean I can't be angry all the time, Nakadai, that takes effort. And making an effort to believe in God is something I don't want to believe in. So I have to focus on the negative; there's no negative in you. That's why I'd probably die around you. I couldn't bear to be around you; I can barely stand writing this fucking letter. But the more I'm bound to others—jealously, resentment, fear—the more I'm certain God doesn't exist. Except he must. Or she must. They. Never makes much sense saying, "They". I digress, but you understand. I've established that already.

Now, the good news: there are times when I distance myself from evil, and the happiness makes God disappear. There's certainly no God when I'm happy. I'd like to die when I'm happy—I know you understand. But then I run back to the anger, I can't imagine being Godless, and the certainty of God returns. It's like I could touch him. But I hate everything he/she/it's created... Then Nakadai's eyes are torn away. "Professor?"

He jolts awake, still in his office, the window looking out on Arkham Main's court. "Hmm?"

"We were going to talk about my introduction?" prods Nicola.

"Introduction to what?"

"My thesis."

"Which draft?"

"Number two."

"Oh yes, the two. Nicola, Nicola. Take a seat."

Nicola sits down wearing a scarf around her neck. It's cold.

"So what did you think?" Nicola asks.

The window brightens Nakadai's baldness. Very bald. He scratches the underside of his chin as though he were in *The Duenna*; that sterling comic opera from Thomas Linley & Co.

"It's doing a lot of introducing," he says.

She sighs. "You didn't read it. Why don't tutors read anything?"

"You don't need to be sceptical around me. I'm not Barthes, for God's sakes." He looks at the email from Captain Khuhro. "I'm sorry, I'm a little preoccupied."

"You're always preoccupied."

"And thank God for preoccupation! I'm *happy* about that, I'm not sure I can say the same for...Nicola, why don't you look at this?"

He points at his screen. She gets up bashfully and stares. She reads the email, examines and deconstructs like the competent linguist she is. "What's he talking about?"

His eyes light up, feline eyes. "You'd think he'd mention his faith. If he's a Buddhist, why doesn't he say that?"

"No God in Buddhism, Nakadai. We're all potential Buddhas, remember?"

"But it's odd, he keeps saying I'd understand. He keeps swinging from hatred to happiness, talking about it. Wouldn't *you* be happy if you were close to God?"

"Suppose God *is* pangender? It'll drive the gender-people crazy. But it's for the greater good."

"Or maybe it's knowing God *is* real," Nakadai postulated privately. "Having certainty about the whole thing. You've got a little Wittgenstein in your thesis, don't you?"

"If we're going to understand God through essence, then what we're taking issue with isn't a thing. It's just essence. So Wittgenstein is free to say whatever he likes."

Nakadai decides against taking Nicola on a day trip. That would be bad practice; putting her in danger and all that. The prospect dots his sizeable mind like Mozart did Tchaikovsky's when he was arranging his *Mozartiana*, however.

He scratches the underside of his chin, again. "He says he can't imagine being Godless, but that's not true—"

"You're acting like a bassoon player."

"Colourful simile."

"Colourful email. You're freaked out, aren't you?"

"I'm sorry," Nakadai shakes his head, "I should focus on you."

"Yes."

He titters. He closes his eyes, thinks a little, and says, "The introductory section. Swap Culpeper for

Yågosh. That should make it more up-to-date. Apart from that, it's fine."

Nicola sighs. She didn't even take off her rucksack. "Thanks, Nakadai."

"No problem. Keep the faith." Then she goes out and slams the door.

Seeing the need to trace over his history with Captain Khuhro, he books a train for Hull and trundles off the following day.

The rain gets heavier the further he moves away from Twickley. He brings *Inspector Miller and the Elasmobranch Banker* for the train journey, he reads from cover to cover the adventures of one *Inspector Miller*, that badass literary detective who rights the wrongs, and wrongs those who would not be right—in this case a crooked banker stealing money from a Catholic Nunnery.

Seeing the station materialize outside, Nakadai eventually steps off the train and trundles to the driverless cab rank. He gets in one, flicks the prawn-flavoured condom off the seat, and says, "The Naval Base, please." A black box beeps and produces a receipt. Nakadai files it away in his wallet, he'll claim on expenses if his name isn't Hiroshi Nakadai, Professor of Neo-Linguistics.

The cab drives itself through the sorry-looking streets of Hull where addicts (white-collar and blue-collar) parade themselves up and down each avenue, crossing crossings, waving cabs down and looking sorrowfully at their feet. (Where is Pierre Gaveaux's *Le Réveil du peuple* when they need to hear it?) Nakadai's cab finally pulls up alongside a huge corrugated fence surrounding what must be the Naval Base. He thanks the "driver" and steps outside, his feet slapping through puddles to the security office as the now-empty cab pulls away.

Nakadai knocks on the little door. A face inside stirs and opens it. A young soldier, clean-shaven, a few spots here and there. "Who the hell are you?"

"My name is Nakadai, I lecture at the University of Twickley."

"Alright, what do you want here?"

Nakadai grins amiably: "Yesterday, I got an email from *Captain Thomas Khuhro*?" He leans in. "It was very distressing."

Much to his immature annoyance, the young soldier twigs instantly. He tries not to give anything away. But this one's *smart*... "Are you a relative?"

"I'm a friend," Nakadai answers. "He did email me. I thought I might find him here."

"He's not here sir." The soldier bristles. He could never be a *heroic tenor*. "But Colonel Redbatch is, I'm afraid—I mean I'm *afraid* I'll have to *report* you to Colonel Redbatch, sir."

"Oh, thank you."

Everything Nakadai does between the security gate and the dull corridors of the base confirms that academics are completely potty: they go through metal detectors, physical searches, Nakadai has to turn out his pockets and what fun *that* is...All the while Nakadai spots the same logo everywhere: *Muton Industries*. He keeps smiling as he finally gets introduced to Colonel Redbatch in his office.

"So..." Colonel Redbatch fills a pipe with tobacco. "You're Professor Nakadai, are you?"

"Yes, I am."

The grizzled Redbatch grumbles. "That'll be all, lad."

The young soldier salutes then turns on his heels and marches out.

"Eager to please, these young people." Pounding tobacco down. "Now, when did you say you received the Khuhro's email?"

Nakadai's still wearing his light-slate-grey-coloured jacket. It's soaking wet. "Just yesterday, it was. Frightfully odd message. Lots of stuff about God." He opened his mouth again. "*You're* not religious, are you?"

"No." He handles the pipe meticulously, obsessively—he is a thousand miles away from Jacques Ibert's neoclassical compositions, renowned for their lightness and wit.

Nakadai adds a little force. "Do you know where I might find him?"

Redbatch strikes a match on his uniform's chest. Lighting the pipe, he puffs quietly for a moment, then he waves out the match and says, "I'm going to be curt with you, Nakadai."

"Oh, yes?"

"We don't enjoy your type barging through here." Puffing. "Military's no place for an academic mind."

With affection, not affectation, Nakadai says, "I do so agree...but Captain Khuhro was very brave, as I recall?"

"Was he."

"I came here with some graduate students about eight months ago. We surveyed the language of soldiers, all about politeness, you see? Very interesting work, lots of data...and our guide for those two weeks was Captain Khuhro."

Redbatch says nothing. He just smokes.

"He was very curious about our research. He told me he'd signed up for some experiments himself. I thought that was *very* brave of him."

Redbatch startles. The click of the pipe on his teeth. "Man threw a wobbly. We discharged him. He needed some money, don't they always, so he signed up for whatever he did. None of my business, Nakadai."

A particularly prosperous plume of smoke.

"I don't pretend to like the man. He was rather weak as a matter of fact. Weak men go by the wayside in places like his."

"You mean this naval base is *different* from others?"

"I mean he was *weak*, Nakadai. That's what I'm saying. Whether you bloody well listen is another matter altogether."

Nakadai smiles. "I see...what university was running the experiments?"

Redbatch puffs angrily, then his face seems to relax. He speaks cryptically: "We've got more privates here than we have staff sergeants. It's a damn nuisance."

Gathering he'd signed up for *private experiments*, this changes everything. "You've been very helpful Colonel. I'll show myself out—is that possible?"

"Anything's possible in the Navy, Nakadai." He spies the little man as he gets up, opens the door, walks into the hallway, then gently shuts the door behind him.

Clamping the pipe between his teeth, Redbatch presses a green button on a video link: *Muton Industries* proudly fills the screen for a second, then a metallic voice:

"This is Muton Industries, how may I help?"

"Hello," he says stiffly, aware he's speaking to a machine, "I need to speak with Dame Bobak."

"Dame Bobak is unavailable."

"Then make her available. She's got trouble, I can't stop it."

The metallic voice seemed to sigh. *"One moment please..."*

A little while after a body is found in the harbour. The harbourmaster calls the police, they rock up wearing white hazmat suits. There's the usual mixture of professionalism and gallows humour as the body is fetched from the grey water. They strap it to a gurney, not that it's going anywhere, and bring it back to the station. The coroner, an older woman with red hair, examines the body and brings the policemen assigned to the case in to have a look.

Inspector Drummond and Sergeant Malpas don't know each other very well. They seem to misjudge the size of the other's feet constantly, bumping awkwardly against an arm or a leg. Drummond explains that Captain Khuhro was stationed at the local Naval Base up until eight months prior. After a mental breakdown, he was discharged. The only other contact Khuhro had was with an academic from the University of Twickley, via email, and sent from one of the public libraries. Then, as if in defence of the body, the coroner says, "The subject died three hours ago. There's no bruising around the body, which suggests he wasn't forced into water. Apart from the water in his lungs, he's a perfect specimen."

"A very *dead* specimen," Malpas says.

"And *why* is he dead?" The coroner points out two scars on the dull shaved head. "An entry-point at the bridge of the nose—another one at the top of the skull. Now, if you follow the two points to a ninety-degree angle inside the brain, you end up in the amygdala: the emotion centre. And this is where it gets even better: judging from the scarring, I'd say surgery took place between eight and seven months ago. Probably around the time he was discharged."

Drummond conceals a terrific cynicism. "A lobotomy?"

"That's the frontal lobe. This is far more delicate."

"Are you saying they took out part of his brain?"

"Or put something *in*." She grabs an X-ray photo and clips it to the glow box.

Both policemen gasp. Malpas screws up his face, "Sir, look! It's a chip or something!"

"I'm afraid it *is* a microchip," the coroner decided. "And I'm *afraid* that's where the trail ends."

"Try me," Drummond says hopefully.

And outside, down the hall, to the left is the station's reception: a cluster of mangled bodies, screaming children and strange otherworldly men crouched in corners wishing they were sipping something a little more than medicinal. This is not a place where Pachelbel's ninety-five fugues based upon the *Magnificat* would have any lasting impact.

Distressed, Nakadai wanders into the station. At the reception he explains everything to a pleasant woman called Joana. She explains they've found a body in the harbour who's been identified as one Thomas Khuhro.

"What's your name again?" Joana asked.

"It's Nakadai. I'm from the University of Twickley."

"*Hiroshi*?"

"Yes, Hiroshi, I don't see why that matters?"

"You were the last person to be in contact with him—*allegedly*. If could just ask you to wait for a moment, I'm sure Inspector Drummond would be happy to talk to you—"

So Nakadai waits, the gaggle around him disturbing and hilarious in equal measure. A few prostitutes wander in demanding the immediate execution of their handcuffed client. When Joana asks them what he did, they draw a square with their fingers. Nakadai shudders.

The burly Drummond wallops down the hall to reception, touches base with Joana, then looks squarely at Nakadai sat disconsolately on the cheap upholstery. He wanders over: "Are you Nakadai?"

"Yes. I assume your name's Drummond?"

"May I ask what you're doing in Hull, sir?"

"I was looking for Captain Khuhro. But I've been informed the man's dead." There was a great, powerful sadness emptying itself into Nakadai's eyes. "I assume you want to ask me things?"

"I think you may be able to help us." Drummond seems to lift Nakadai from his seat and they go to his office, a shabby functional room with a few chairs and a desk, in another part of the building. Introductions are made, then Nakadai shows them the email he received. First Malpas reads it, then Drummond. Both men's eyes fluctuate between disbelief and cruel laughter. Drummond is the first to speak: "You say you met him just the once?"

"I have one of those faces," Nakadai says glumly.

"There's something you should know."

"Well, spit it out then."

Taken aback by the sudden anger in the man's voice, Drummond says, "For the past seven months the deceased caused a great many public disturbances. They may have been minor offences but he got a reputation."

Nakadai looks at the plain floor. "Was he ever arrested?"

Malpas says, "A few times. But we always let him off."

"You mean he wasn't *worth* charging?"

"In a manner of speaking—"

"In *plain* speaking, sergeant, what was he getting up to?"

Drummond cut in: "He'd kick up a fuss in the supermarket. That sort of thing."

"*Be specific inspector*...what was this man doing *specifically*? In plain speaking?"

"He would go up to people."

"Which people? How did he choose them?"

"He was good at picking fights. He just couldn't get the size right. Any time the police showed up he was fighting someone bigger than him. Men, women, it didn't matter. He'd be throwing things, swearing, anything to piss them off."

"He probably did it on purpose."

Drummond starts mocking him: "Why would he do it on purpose?"

"I don't know inspector!" Nakadai shouted. Then he gathered himself. "What does the email say? *What is this private hell I'm in?* It's not a public hell, it's private. It's got nothing to do with other people; he's *fighting* them because there's something not quite right inside..." The policemen shift uneasily. They try not to trade glances, but they do and Nakadai watches everything with a kind of feline stupor. "Of course," he began quietly, "There might've been something *literally* wrong with his head..."

They agree to take him to the coroner's lab, he goes in ahead of them and greets the coroner whose hands are bloody from an examination of Captain Khuhro's brain. He shakes her red hands excitedly, looks down in surprise, then says, "Don't worry, I'm not adverse to butcher shops!"

He stumbles through the rest of the lab as Drummond and Malpas try to coax the coroner out of her indignation at the strange little man examining everything but the body.

"This is *not* a butcher shop," she says as though she were singing in Vivaldi's *Oratorio*, "and do be careful, don't get anything dirty—"

"I won't—" He stops dead over the body. The head is sewn up like a vulgar doll, and put back together again before its owner shoves it in the wash. Like a massive grapefruit caught in some textile factory, the semblance of bone poking out from the rugged skin, a bad joke. "Oh, dear." He looks up at the coroner who is staring impetuously at him. "You said you found something. May I see it?" Exhaling, she picks up a shining kidney dish with something metal covered in blood and places it before him.

Nakadai says, "Now, stay back all of you, don't touch it." Malpas covers his mouth, about to puke. "It may not be dormant yet."

The coroner raises her eyebrow. "Dormant?"

"You don't put dead things in people's heads. If you're going to make them act differently, affect a change in them, you're going to need something alive." He frowns. "And Thomas, like the chip, was very much alive."

Malpas coughs. "Not anymore."

"Yes, I gathered that." He looks at Drummond. "You said he'd been arrested. He must've had an address, what was it?"

Transfixed by the chip, he says, "He was living on Holland Street. When he couldn't pay the rent, they chucked him out. He was living at the homeless shelter towards the end. They chucked him out too, he kept picking fights with the other homeless people."

"He didn't have a smartphone, did he?"

"No."

"Good chap." Nakadai pauses. "How did he send the email?"

"Public library. We checked; they'd never seen him before. I suppose he was banking on you."

"It rather looks that way, doesn't it?"

The Professor of Neo-Linguistics looks at the ceiling for a moment, deep in thought. He is caught in something big, far beyond a single Naval Base in the north of England, then there is the catch: there he is, caring about someone who's died in one of the most deprived parts of the country, something the true perpetrator hadn't expected in the least...

In the tallest building in London, two people are quickly catching onto that fact. One of them has sold out, but the other is extremely peeved about the whole business. The first is Colonel Redbatch, he is sitting awkwardly in a cramped metal chair that is too small for him and, crucially, *not* smoking his pipe.

The other is a stark-looking woman with high eyebrows called Dame Bobak. She not only owns the building, but also the entire interconnected network of sales and shares which constitute Muton Industries. Like a nineteenth-century rhapsody, her empire is generally free in form and shares those elements which made the Roman Empire so powerful—and eventually crumble.

In her hands is a rather delicate, but deadly, letter-opener running up and down her lithe fingers, which gives Colonel Redbatch the willies.

"Who is he?" she asks with supreme authority. After all, it's her office, not his.

"He's called Nakadai—"

"I know his name already. Who is he?"

Redbatch is out of ideas. "I don't know."

She rolls her eyes in full view of her guest, then puts the letter-opener back in its holder on the edge of the desk. Redbatch forces out that Nakadai knew Captain Khuhro; now he appears to be cooperating with the police. "God knows," he adds.

Bobak stands up and looks through the enormous window looking out onto Clapham. It used to be such a drab place, Clapham, but that was before Bobak came with industry, concrete and jobs. She practically owns Clapham. Putting this bizarre victory to one side, she says, "I've always had the suspicion that people in the military don't care nearly enough about providence."

"I blame boarding school," Redbatch replies. "Not a lot of God in the English boarding school, I must say. Quite a bore actually; but the bore puts the fear of God in you. The staff are God. The people that maintain your house. The older boys, the bastards." He sniggers. "I never could see the benefits of leprosy."

Uneasy because his host isn't saying anything, he pours himself a glass of water from the table. Something strong and stable about a jug of water on a desk. Something official, and trusty about it. He sips quietly and precisely, clearing his throat.

What he doesn't know is in the laboratories beneath the building is a balding, middle-aged man called Dr. Phineas Fernsby who hasn't slept properly in a year and is wondering whether the chemical conditioning he's worked so hard on will affect

Colonel Redbatch. His whole life resembles a *Ländler*, a slow waltz practiced in Austria before *waltz proper* swept the continent and others.

The empty glass hits the table. "I don't suppose you like cricket?"

Dame Bobak turns round to see if the conditioning starts immediately. She is sorely disappointed when he keeps going on about cricket. "Wonderful sport!"

"Colonel, where did they find Khuhro?"

"In the harbour." He conceals two guilts: one for her, the other for the deceased. "He drowned himself."

"Pity..." She stands eerily close to him like she is taking in every single detail of his body. "I want you to bring this Nakadai to me."

Redbatch gets up, leaking disapproval: "You can't just snap your fingers! There's a protocol for everything. I'll have to get in touch with the police, the police will get in touch with you. You can't possibly *want* that sort of attention *now*?"

"I know. But I want you to bring this Nakadai to me."

"I can't..." The words stick in his throat. "I...will..." He shakes his head, squeezing the bridge of his nose with jittery old fingers. He suddenly thinks to himself: *I really want to say something*: "I'll bring Nakadai here. I'll take him back when you're finished with him."

Pleased with Fernsby's progress, Bobak smiles and says, "I knew you'd see things my way. Before you go, though, I must ask: Did you betray me, colonel?"

"Yes," he speaks in a droll manner. "I hinted at your involvement because I resent you immensely. Not because you're a woman, but because you hurt people. But I will bring Nakadai here. I'll take him back when you're finished with him."

"Please leave." She touches a green button on her desk. Downstairs Fernsby steps into view, he can see his potion at work.

"I...obey..." Redbatch walks calmly out of the room. Bobak looks at Fernsby on the video link and smiles. "You've done well, Fernsby. It works."

"I can't g-guarantee the span of the c-conditioning. It may w-w-wear—"

"Wear off? We'll see." She chuckles. "We'll see how long before your luck runs out, Phineas. Now, back to play..." She clicks off before he can reply, then frowns with mounting displeasure at the state of the world. With a brain like Nakadai's, she may find God after all.

Colonel Redbatch returns to Hull via helicopter, re-enters his office and begins to mount an offensive on Nakadai and Khuhro. He is *Katerina* in Shostakovich's *Katerina Ismailova*—but this murderous tale does not run a risk, under Redbatch's supervision, of being banned by Stalin. The young soldier from before is called in, given strict instructions to keep his interactions with Nakadai a secret, then sent marching, along with every member of personnel who vetted the professor on his way in. A general announcement is made, blocking exits, siphoning control away from the various sectors and into Colonel Redbatch's office. Next, he calls his trusted confidante, Second Lieutenant Kapoor, into the unhappy room. He reels off a series of instructions that don't make sense and then gives the ultimate one: "The police tell me Hiroshi Nakadai is about to leave the city. You will bring him here for interrogation."

Kapoor has known the colonel for years. He can be arrogant and sycophantic, but never something approaching senile. "You want this Nakadai *arrested*, sir?"

A blank, disinterested response: "Are you questioning my authority?"

"No sir. I just don't know where to begin."

"I...understand where you're coming from lieutenant." A struggle with some foreign power. "We've got photos from the police. He's a dangerous man. That is why we must arrest him."

"With all due respect sir, if the police know he's headed off, why don't *they* arrest him?"

"This is a military matter! You will obey!" He passes a Muton Industries-manufactured tablet to the quivering, baffled lieutenant. He swipes through the photos of Nakadai, all of them from low angles, like they're all stills taken from some obscure French film. Having already overstayed his welcome, Kapoor salutes the colonel and turns on his heels, exiting the office. On his way to an official car, an equally nervous Private Green in tow, he realizes the colonel's pipe was just sitting on the desk, untouched. The colonel's had that pipe since his glory days at Sandhurst: he never makes a decision without a few trusty puffs. Losing time, he pockets these problems and gets in the car with Private Green. They squeal out of the complex toward the train station, the rain gathering speed as they are.

Meanwhile, Nakadai's struggling with the ticket barrier. Some un-tired member of personnel helps Nakadai through. He goes to Platform 3 and stands around waiting. The air is yellow, like something out of a Russian novel. He has the strange feeling he's being watched. "More Czech," Nakadai says under his breath. He scans the platform and sees a woman pretending to look at train times: her name is Private Green and watches Nakadai watching *her*. Time to strike.

Seeing he's in trouble, he starts for the station shop only to find a man wearing a beanie is starting for *him*: Lieutenant Kapoor watches Private Greena and they together watch Nakadai half-jog into the foyer and shove his ticket through the ticket barrier, which doesn't work. Floods of angry people accrue; they're trying to get out and he's being obstructive. The same un-tired member of personnel listens to Nakadai's health-related excuse, then lets him through and watches Private Green and Lieutenant Kapoor force their way through the barriers.

In the meantime, Nakadai runs to the nearest cab where he is pulled away by a pair of huge hands to an *unmarked* car. He's thrown in the back and finds himself looking at Inspector Drummond. "Hello, professor."

The driver puts his foot through the floor and the car zips off. They go down roads and up ramps, watching the swirling pools of car-suffocated tarmac below them. Nakadai asks: "Have you been following me?"

"That goes without saying. Doesn't it, Neil?"

Malpas in the front seat: "It does, sir."

"We've been following the people following you. You're quite popular." He squints, taking note of the road. "Don't ask why."

"Who are they?"

"Colonel Redbatch sent them. He doesn't strike me as the type to lend out His Majesty's vehicles. And what *crap* vehicles they are."

"Oh, yes?" Nakadai puffs. "What am I going to do, inspector?"

"Sir—" Malpas reflected in the mirror. "We've got company."

They're on a dual carriage-way. The car lurches to the left.

(Drummond buckles Nakadai's seatbelt without his consent.)

Kapoor's car follows, weaving between pedestrian vehicles, delivery trucks and the odd ice-cream van.

Kapoor accelerates forward and Malpas takes his foot off the pedal. Their bumpers collide and both parties jolt inside their vehicles.

A sixteen-wheeler lay ahead, the only respite Malpas can see. He presses the pedal down, the engine whirs louder and louder. The driver of the immense truck sees what's coming and decreases speed, almost squishing Kapoor's car into an ice-cream van. Luckily (or unluckily) Kapoor keeps up with the car he's tailing and pulls alongside.

Drummond tells Nakadai to lower himself and his window. He pulls out his gun and shoots directly into the car opposite. Kapoor and Green flail their arms and the car swings out of control and breaks through a railing, striking the side of a stationary caravan parked in the grassy bit adjacent to the carriageway. The car does not explode but Kapoor and Green know that someone, undoubtedly with a higher pay grade, will.

On the Naval Base, there is pandemonium. Colonel Redbatch is found slumped over his desk by that young soldier. He revives him with cognac and the ballet music of Kan Ishii. (Who would have thought Colonel Redbatch liked ballet?)

Redbatch is like a sieve when he wakes up. He can't remember anything he's done in the past twelve hours. When he's told the truth the colonel becomes volcanic, stuffing his pipe with tobacco and puffing heatedly for ten minutes. He sniffs and countermands every order he's given up to that point. He apologises personally to each member of personnel who vetted Nakadai; he revokes all announcements he made prior, then unblocks the exits he blocked. Happy to see the base ticking like clockwork again, Redbatch goes a plum colour and presses the green button on his video link.

When Dame Bobak answers the call, it's clear the colonel has reverted to his anti-religious and pro-establishment stances. He's worse than usual: *"I don't remember discussing Nakadai with you!"* he shouts down the video link. *"Why on earth would I agree to arrest him? I've never heard such rubbish! You're losing your marbles, Ruth!"*

Bobak personifies the innocence and frustration found in Bach's *Coffee Cantata*. She leans back in her high-backed chair, looking down her sharp nose at him: "I'm sorry to hear you think that, colonel. There must be a misunderstanding *somewhere—*"

"Now I hear one of my men is injured, and he tells me it was my idea to go on this wild goose chase in the first place! I told him he was stark-raving mad. He hasn't got a clue about protocol. But that's by-the-by: you stay away from my base, do you hear? If I catch you prowling around my neck of the woods, I'll get you!"

She lowers her glance, her face collecting the sunlight reflected off of Clapham: "Are you threatening me, colonel?"

"I bloody well am! You keep that rich nose of yours out of my business!"

He ends the call. No one ends a call with Dame Bobak. If she doesn't end the call, you could be talking to her for the rest of your life. (Some of Phineas Fernsby's longest conversations have been with Bobak; the rest have been with his mother—a lisping Liverpudlian with jaundice. Not that Bobak takes any interest in her employees' families' lives.) She pounds the desk with her hands, then prepares herself for an interview on the BBC. They're giving her a hard time about the tax her company *doesn't* pay. Indeed, one of the things working both in her favour and against her is how human nature never changes. Not unless it's provoked with a sharp liquor, a powdered substance, or a microchip.

Back in Hull the police bring in a North American specialist called Martha Ruler to examine the microchip the coroner yanked out of Captain Khuhro's brain. She wears thick glasses and speaks with a Bostonian accent, maybe even an air of excitement when they bring her the shining kidney dish in the coroner's lab. She spends a great deal of time examining it, prodding it, making notes on her smartphone, laughing from scientific ecstasy and then pity.

She turns to Drummond, Malpas, the coroner and Nakadai and says, "It's something like a mix between an antidepressant and a SIM card—*may he rest in peace.*"

Nakadai glowers at the kidney dish. He articulates, massages and composes thoughts like a sonnet, scene or a short precise novel. He calls back the email, clicking the lens of his mind to the right level of focus: "*But the more I'm bound to others—jealously, resentment, fear—the more I'm certain God doesn't exist.*"

Nakadai perks up: "An addiction."

Martha has been babbling on for some time and the interruption catches her off-guard. "A what?"

"When he was angry, he was able to find God. But when he was content, when he was happy, there was nothing—and no one. So he became addicted to the anger; the potential for God. It was necessary, he *thought* it was necessary, so he became addicted." He walks through them as he's speaking. "He couldn't deny himself God; who would? Therefore, he couldn't deny himself the anger he required to have a God."

In that parabolic tone that North Americans use—and much to the fury of the realists in the room—Martha concludes: "He was addicted to God-certainty. And so, the certainty of there being a God is what drove him to suicide. Because when he was happy, he was Godless, but when he'd *found* God, he was inhospitable to mankind."

(Malpas rolls his eyes; he is most definitely the peasant in Suppé's *Poet and Peasant.*)

The microchip's function, and what Dr. Phineas Fernsby had accomplished, were quite remarkable. It had forced Captain Khuhro to choose between, on the one hand, his devotion to God, and on the other hand, his membership in the animal kingdom. It was, in that sense, the essence of the Catholic Church mapped onto an electronic membrane. A powerful weapon.

Martha adds, "But the binary lends itself to incompetence rather than intelligent design."

Malpas clears his throat. "You mean it's knackered?"

"The point of the microchip, on paper, is a singularity: to feel that amazing God-certainty no matter how you feel. It has one job, you could say. But if something *frustrates* that job there's nothing you can do about it. I guess, then, like an antibody fighting bacteria in the bloodstream, Captain Khuhro's brain fought back."

"And lost," Nakadai says.

She agrees, and together they mourn the man whose body, at that very moment, is chilled to the point of stasis in a steel locker adjacent to them. Rows and rows of people, chilled to keep, and yet how many of them had the bravery of Captain Khuhro?

Dame Bobak knows he'll come. She stands in her office, waiting. Not prone to self-reflection, she stuns herself when suddenly memories come flooding back. How she started Muton Industries in her bedroom at Loughborough University. How she fought to keep control when, after financial success, she found herself surrounded by board members whose sole intent was to make money. Dame Bobak doesn't care about money. Her ideas span larger cerebral car parks than your average tech-guru. She remembers telling them her intentions of finding the God-essence, a human factor that would revolutionize every social media application she'd invented, watched over, was intent on perpetuating *ad infinitum*. When they laughed her out of her boardroom, she fired them all. Now she's in sole control, making her dreams a reality; and the ultimate reality, she thinks, is the re-education of the human race.

A buzz on her desk. Hovering over her video link, she presses the green button. Her bawdy male receptionist, Charlie, says there's a Professor Hiroshi Nakadai to see her.

"I've been expecting him. Send him up, Charlie, there's a good boy." She smiled. "*Alone*, Charlie."

She ends that interaction and starts another one. In the bowels of the building, in the Muton Industries laboratories, Dr. Phineas Fernsby sits in front of a microchip. The magnification glass he's using is pricked with drops of sweat. He's been working on what's meant to be the improved microchip for months now. Apart from the mind-control garbage, this thing has taken up all his time. He's barely been able to see his lisping Liverpudlian mother—and he's starting to crack. He answers, barely, the video link. "Y-Yes, ma'am?"

"How lucky are we today, Phineas?"

"N-N-No comment."

"Tough. Is the improved microchip ready?"

Phineas stirs, a thousand legal ramifications mapping his mind like a child's kaleidoscope. "Yes," he lies, "b-but I w-wouldn't—"

"Excellent, Phineas. Bring it up immediately." She smiles in the video. *"With the surgical team. We're moving ahead, Phineas."*

After she curtly stops the call with her mentally dismembered head scientist, a light glows above the door. Dame Bobak remains seated at her desk. She looks briefly at the deadly letter-opener resting in its holder. "Enter."

Nakadai walks into the office. He purposefully ignores her and walks over to the window. It looks as though his light-slate-grey-coloured jacket is still wet from his first day in Hull. He's not one for ornaments; on his face or anywhere else, for that matter.

"So," Bobak begins, "you're Nakadai, are you?"

Nakadai turns round. "You were expecting someone else?"

"*No*," she replied suspiciously, "I wasn't. We're being joined by a few others in a short moment. You're not against mingling, I hope?"

"Not in principle."

"Good. Take a seat. Would you like some water?"

"I prefer to stand. I'm not thirsty."

"Suit yourself." His head is outlined by the dying light outside. The dying, reflected light of Clapham. "You've caused me a considerable amount of trouble, Nakadai."

He says happily, "I'm not particularly interested in your woes."

"Nor am I. I don't think I have any." She looks him up and down. "*Certainly none to spare*. Why are you here?"

"Colonel Redbatch. You know him." He cuts her off. "You hated him. He was an arrogant bastard.

He wasn't beyond a crisis of conscience, however. You probably should have put the chip in him; you would've saved yourself a lot of trouble."

"What trouble?"

"The trouble of taking life."

She chuckles matter-of-factly, "Captain Khuhro knew the risks. He didn't have to sign the contract and he didn't have to end up how he did. The medication was *recommended*—"

"I don't think paracetamol would've done him a world of good, do you?"

"I'm no expert—"

"Then why behave like one?"

The feedback from several security cameras dots the underbelly of Bobak's desk. She pretends to look down and sees policemen flooding the area outside the central lobby. Charlie will deal with them in his way. But she's running out of time. She says, "You know the University of Twickley offered me an honourary doctorate? I just gave them a lot of money instead—"

"That's very generous. But I doubt my employers would do business with someone after they'd been investigated for breaches in ethical code by the Ministry of Technology."

"That bunch of chuckleheads would strip your hyde as quickly as they would mine."

"That's *probably* why I work for them."

She goes pale. "What?"

"They don't like getting their hands dirty: they're a bit like you." Seeing the change of colour on Bobak's face, he proceeds to walk scholastically around the room. "They've been following your advancements in wireless therapy. They want them *stopped* immediately..."

Whether she's angry at Phineas for being slow, or at Nakadai for being right, is difficult to tell. Her lips tremble in vexation and she stands up as her guest continues: "Quite apart from all that a man has been murdered—"

"He committed suicide!" Dame Bobak shouts back. "You know that, everyone does! Why do you persist in pretending!"

"There's a difference between falling off a cliff, *and being pushed!*"

On the other side of the room, a secret panel slides away to reveal a separate door. The door slides open and Phineas walks in with a gurney, surgical equipment plus a team of medically-minded hoodlums. They look as though they should be accompanied by an *ocarina*.

Phineas does a double-take at Nakadai: "Oh my God! He's s-still standing up!"

Bobak screams, "Shut up, Phineas! Now get him on there! I want you to start the operation immediately!" The surgeons, clearly not so bothered by their ethical standards, race over to Nakadai and grab him, shoving him on the gurney. They strap him down like a wild animal: cold white leather squeaks against his still-damp light-slate-grey-coloured jacket. Phineas objects at full volume, a monument to everything irritating and true. He pushes himself away from the surgical preparations and mewls next to Bobak.

Except she can't hear him: she's taken with the revenge, the scheming, the endless plotting of her incessant unhappy life.

"Is this completely necessary?" Nakadai blubbers as the surgeons tighten the straps to a snapping point. "I can't breathe!" He sees a surgeon preparing a series of intravenous needles. "You're insane! You must stop this!"

Phineas gets on his knees. He tugs at Dame Bobak's pant suit. "P-Please! He's right! We can't work w-without his c-consent!"

"Get off me, Phineas! I'm going to go downstairs and deal with the police."

The word sends shivers through the emasculated man's body. "P-P-P-P-Police! We haven't got a chance! They'll c-come up here and arrest everyone!"

Dame Bobak collects the letter-opener from her desk in a furious fit of maladjusted senses. Phineas attempts to pry the bone-saw from the surgeon's hands. "MOM, I'M SORRY!" She stabs the blade straight into his back; he grunts in pain then falls dead on the imported carpet.

Bobak tells the surgeons to hurry up. Nakadai shouts in horror as the bone-saw is switched on and his wrist prepared for needle insertion—

Drummond and Malpas burst through the door with ten other policemen. They shoot the ceiling just above Nakadai and pieces of plaster fall on him. "What are you doing!"

"Ruth Bobak," Inspector Drummond interjects, "I'm arresting you on counts of payroll and recruitment fraud. You do not have to say anything, but it may harm your defence if you do not mention when questioned something which you later rely on in court. Anything you do say may be given in evidence. Do you understand everything I've just said to you?"

Bobak seems to disappear. There is barely anything left of that promising brain from Brexton University. *"Yes."*

Two police—one bearded, the other female—put Bobak and her surgeons in handcuffs and take them downstairs for the kind of reckoning heard during the explosive conclusion of Verdi's *Falstaff*. Drummond and Malpas unstrap Nakadai from the gurney. The inspector watches the professor rubbing his arms where the straps were tightest, panting as though he has just finished *listening* to Verdi's *Falstaff*. "Are you alright?"

Nakadai sucks his teeth. "Not the best timing, inspector."

"You said fifteen minutes—"

"Ten! You can't tell the difference between fifteen and ten? Good, God! How I *weep* for England!" He changes tack quickly. "I don't care if the court hears that part." He pulls a voice recorder out of his jacket pocket, hands it to Drummond and straightens the damp jacket covering his beating heart. "There should be enough to indict her. That and Dr. Fernsby. *Poor* Dr. Fernsby. I would appreciate it if you let *me* call his mother."

Drummond frowns. "Why?"

"Because I feel sorry for him."

A hand is placed on Nakadai's shoulder. "Thank you. For all the help."

"I'm not sure if you're welcome, inspector. But time will tell..."

Nakadai leaves the building and dodges the ramshackle photographic crowd, the dying sunlight blistering the tops of buildings and saying goodbye to the people on the street, not that they take any notice of this. He sees Malpas, briefly, trying to convince a local officer into giving him a cigarette. He puts them out of his mind and zig-zags through the badly-parked cars belonging to police personnel and journalists. A few punters, here and there. He recalls from memory that strangest part of Captain Khuhro's letter, an elegy for the raining day and the ding of an email:

There's a climber. There's a climber and he's climbing and he falls. He doesn't fall to his death, if you get what I'm saying; what I mean is he's falling and falling, for so long he doesn't know which way is up. He may be falling up. You're reading this, I can tell you understand, I can feel it ripping through...

Here endeth the tale which constitutes the original impressions that my doctoral tutor made upon me. With those happenings out of the way, I would like ideally to continue with and terminate the narrative I set myself the task of penning in the first instance. I have made myself an instant coffee and am probably damaging the abnormal cells which later may become cancer. Puccini's *Madame Butterfly* is playing in the background and I feel subconsciously caught up in the story; whenever I listen to this particular opera, I have the faintest feeling that Cio-Cio-San may, perhaps, *not* commit suicide. (To those who have never experienced *Madame Butterfly*, I apologize.)

Nakadai's second book, *The Word Machine*, was more or less finished. The book's state was clear to me when I met Nakadai for one-on-one meetings. He looked unconditionally drained and downright debilitated.

> I must confess that during those first meetings of ours, I felt that I would die imminently and leave you the unpleasant task of finishing your PhD without a primary tutor; not that Goro would've been unhelpful in his capacity as your secondary tutor. He would have taken over for me, doubtless. But I was aware that I was not long for this world—but I had a task to perform, nonetheless, and I was determined to perform it, no matter the cost.

This was when, in his capacity as the Professor of Neo-Linguistics, he asked me if I would like to cover his seminars. His enquiry left me agape in terror given the amount of work I would need to undertake to teach the requisite modules.

He assured me that it wasn't that difficult and that a monkey could teach a university seminar. He said that university tutors tended to regurgitate like flies the knowledge they had digested over the years; that their lessons were not dissimilar in this respect. Likewise, Mengelberg repeatedly conducted the compositions of Beethoven and Mahler—until, of course, he was banned from conducting in the Netherlands due to his Nazi sympathies which, incidentally, is one of the few ways, Nakadai assured me, you could get fired from a university.

"It's essential that you do this," Nakadai said, speaking not about Mengelberg, but about my taking on his teaching. "It's the only way that I can complete *my* tasks, do you see? Of course, you are in no way obliged to accept my offer..."

This was not bullying so much as bribing. If prospective universities were aware in the future that, before I sat my final *viva voce*, I had taught the Introduction to Neo-Linguistics (NL1311), Neo-Linguistic Theory (NL1315) and Grammatical Philosophy (NL1318) modules—they would probably give serious thought to hiring me on the spot. It would be like Jean-Baptiste Moreau claiming to have played with John Coltrane and Charles Mingus—even though Moreau lived 300 years before Coltrane and Mingus had even been born.

This mighty triumvirate of modules was known as The Three Modules of Death as their complexity and philosophical ambition were without equal. There were not many who would be brave enough—or stupid enough—to even *begin* to undertake the reading required to teach these modules. But I was young and brash and more preoccupied with my brilliant career than with reality. Was Alice Coltrane preoccupied with reality when she wrote *Transcendence*? Was Ruth Crawford preoccupied with reality when she wrote her *String Quartet*? Was Jan Bartos, despite his government posts in music and education, preoccupied with reality when he wrote his five symphonies? And if I taught the aforementioned Modules of Death, wouldn't my career be a bright one? I agreed, unsurprisingly, to take on the teaching that would allow my tutor to get on with his work. I only realized the insanity of this when I got returned to my apartment that evening and put on Satie's *Parade*. I crawled under my duvet and prayed to the God of Linguistics—who is most certainly *not* the Great Word—to help me get through the crazy task I had set myself.

As you might have realized, dear reader, I was not defeated or destroyed by the Three Modules of Death. I rather enjoyed my teaching, on the contrary, and struck fear into several colleagues who had otherwise viewed youth as a handicap prior to my joining their reluctant ranks. Regardless, it was the only time in which I saved Nakadai—for, as the years churned on, it became clear that Nakadai was working to save not only me but the entirety of our creative world...

14

RAW LINGUISTIC MATTER—TATYANA BARYSHEV—DEPOSITION 9962/B—GORO'S GLEE

Nakadai finished building his Word Machine and unveiled it to Mutton in Arkham Main. The unveiling took place, much like Marius Constant's *Paradise Lost* in 1967, at a prespecified time in the evening. It had been raining all day and continued to rain after sunset. Arkham Main's structure was severely dampened and its various grooves and dips were wetted and dried in a cycle of liquefied equilibrium. The internal heating was turned down as Mutton stood in Nakadai's office examining the hard work the shivering Professor had churned out.

> I gave him what he wanted. The Word Machine would not only perform linguistic functions—but also facilitate the widening of reality-related fibres that would eventually permit the Great Word to enter our universe. This would be a *religious experience* for the Great Word as it would change from a state

of *self-centredness* to a state of *reality-centredness*. Professor Mutton and I would bear witness to a new and terrible religious tradition; I was none too pleased about this, however, and shrivelled at my involvement in this decidedly evil process. The Word Machine itself was crabby with leg-like radials pronging into the air. Two large spinning discs were affixed to the sides of the machine with multifarious digits and roman characters and a grammatical mesh was suspended between the two discs in an attempt to filter out every imperfect word the device calculated; akin to an inverted megaphone. Professor Mutton recoiled as though the Word Machine were alive when he touched it with a milky, withered hand. Much in the same way that some Japanese Catholic scholars deny there being a Japanese identity *per se* and favour instead the essentialist body of Catholic doctrine, the Word Machine possessed an inter-cultural quality; it was a living thing that would, in time, draw upon all living things. Having stung himself on the machine, however, Mutton examined his finger cautiously then shot towards me a gaze of steely gratification. He was nervous and, bearing in mind how God had saved Christ and would subsequently save each human life, knew that any release from bondage I experienced would too be turned upon *him*. The artificial prolonging of Mutton's life was about to end. "Now," said Mutton tiredly, "what do you need to make it work? If the *now* were the moment when a clock strikes hardest it would be clanging angrily, ceaselessly, at this very moment! We *must* hurry, Nakadai. What do you need? The Great Word is past, present, future: an *infinite* series and your machine, I hope, requires something infinitely simple to make that so!" He paused a moment. "But never mind all that: what do you need?" This, like whether Japanese Bishops unnecessarily provoked those at the Vatican, was a very reasonable question. I replied calmly that what the machine required was *raw linguistic matter*; something in the region of every known word in English. Mutton looked at me as though I had said the tension between Japanese Bishops and the Vatican was *unhealthy*. (Naturally, I think the opposite.) "What do you think I am?" he replied. 'some famous Circle circulating some famous inflammatory text? Don't command me, Nakadai: I lack your arrogance, your self-serving qualities. We're running out of time, Nakadai, I'm dying like an old way of thinking. Running dry like a reservoir and rising like an ocean and you're content to waste me like some arbitrary fossil fuel. My hands...once so full, powerful...they're nothing but talons now, sucked dry by *your* lack of progress!" The intellectual geography I was working in was, like the spiritual geography of Japan, a swamp where new ideas rarely took root. I told Mutton that, like Francis Xavier, my progress had to mature at the pace set by the geography I found myself in. Then, in what appeared to be a theatrical act of horror, Mutton opened his trench coat and showed off the skeletal, concave frame which had devolved over the years. He laughed and said, "You're like a retired steel magnate pretending to be artistic! I shall enjoy seeing you to the very end of your employment. You won't enjoy it: full of dead children, *Japanese* children...it will be just like the Tsushima War. You'll feel right at home...or have you lost your sympathy with your people? No emotions, no hope, no nothing—I'll be shocked if you outlive *me*!" I explained that his words were like *Fumi-e*—nothing more than thin-skinned methods used to reveal the faith of Japanese Christians; and something which, in my opinion, made their faiths grow stronger. I reminded Mutton that without the Word Machine there would be no Great Word; that without the Great Word there would be no Professor Mutton—not in this current state, anyway. Mutton then hobbled closer and stood an inch away from my face. "Like a superb translation carried out by some malicious student," he hissed, "I see into your soul, Nakadai. Your mind is with me in wake and slumber. Your little memoirs, your fictionalizations, as you call them, are not without interest. I watch them forming; I chuckle at their naïvety. When all is said and done Nakadai withdraws, like the snails in Baryshev's stories, into his protective shell. You think you are different from the others here, but you are not. You are like *them*: suspicious to the point of insanity, locked away from the world, compiling resentments and turning them into groundless theories. Theories without earth. But I shall have *this* earth, at least. The earth will be quite different after that. There'll be no place for Nakadai on *that* earth..." Then once again I stated that I needed raw linguistic matter and that that was the end of the matter. "And you, like a lame-legged proletarian avoiding the draft, shall have it! Your equivalent of wining, dining and gambling! Your thoughts are like Swiss cheese, easy to read and marketable. But should you ever anticipate a rival market, I shall know and discipline you as I did those before you: the missionary who caught flu, the rich boy who gave his money away, the drugged woman who dreamed of a better life. I anticipated your request. You shall have a partner, briefly: a woman of cunning talent whom you'll meet in Twickley Lodge. The one with the druggies outside. Once there, you will explain to her what must be done, and she will do it. Just as my life is in the balance, a philosophy seeking peace, so too is yours. Don't forget that I see into your *soul...*!"

With that, Mutton exited the office and left Nakadai with his Word Machine. The mood made Claudio Merulo's madrigals seem positively cheery. Briefly, in deep silence, he contemplated the meeting he would secretly oversee in a budget hotel in a budget country: namely England. The individual Mutton had hired was a Russian subversive called Tatyana Baryshev who was a medium-sized woman with pluffs of red hair and dense shoulder muscles that showed through cashmere sweaters like erotic mountain ranges. She had been living in the Ural Mountain town of Kungur when Mutton had massaged her ego using the symphonies of Nicolai Miaskovsky.

For a time, Mutton had considered hiring her competitor, Vladimir Shwetz; he was serving two consecutive sentences in Norlisk which, for any novice, was the most polluted city in Russia. Tatyana agreed to receive a hefty university-subsidized payment after her work had been completed, subsequently met with Nakadai in Twickley, received her payment and left the country. It was around this time that, like the sacrifice of King Fisher in *The Midsummer Marriage*, Tatyana was arrested in Japan by their Second Intelligence Department and charged with meddling in the recent general election. In what seemed to be the silent wish of her competitor Shwetz, Tatyana received two consecutive sentences to be carried out in the Asago Women's Correctional Facility. It was during this time that she began to sing as though the prison's chaplain had placed in her hand the most recent *psalter*. She gave an irritating deposition that outlined the exploits of Mutton and his emissary Nakadai. You will appreciate, dear reader, how this deposition was near-impossible to gain access to. I pleaded with the Second Intelligence Department's attaché in London, however, and managed to secure a redacted version of the interview that dealt exclusively with Tatyana's involvement in the infernal, illegal plans of Professor Mutton. Thus, in its stunted entirety, follows the relevant deposition extract.

> William Blake was right about England. *It is a land of poverty!* My plane landed in Manchester and I

caught the train to Twickley. I walked from the train station, observing the *bleak and bare* fields, to Twickley Lodge—this is a place where people carry out extramarital affairs. It suited the meeting perfectly and I knocked at Room No. 62. It was late in the evening and *painted birds* returned from Wetherspoon's and cried in their rooms. My client opened the door and I walked in; I struggled to see because it was dark. It was a room full of *dark disputes* and *artful teasing*—I sat upon a chair and asked who he was. He turned the lights on and I saw that he was Japanese, except he spoke English as well as the *painted birds*—he was a kind of *sham-Anglo-Saxon*, I concluded; a man who had assimilated to his surroundings but who, with a degree of *swaddling bands*, had refused to assimilate *completely*.

He explained how he was under the influence of Professor Mutton; the man who was the real client. Nakadai, as he introduced himself, was merely a kind of emissary for *Mutton*; the man who had hired me for data collection. I was not used to *pleasant streams* in business negotiations. The *sham-Anglo-Saxon* wasted no time on vodka, cigarettes, rye bread and stories. Rather, he explained that he needed data in the form of nouns, verbs, adjectives, adverbs, conjunctions, articles and interjections. Then, as though his mother had taught him *underneath a tree*, he took my hand and said, *Language is pictures—the pictures stop when we die—therefore, language allows us to see until we die.* I thought he looked exhausted and maddening; he was a *bard* who could see the present, past and future *among the ancient trees.* William Blake, however, is not a man you want to work for; he is the kind of man you admire from miles away. Nakadai was undoubtedly with me, though; he went on to say that the data he had outlined was unfixed and would constitute an *opportunistic corpus.* Where would I find such data? Who could provide me with these strange, irrelevant things? His answer seemed to arise from the dewy grass when he said, *The British Traffic Light Surveillance Database.*

Now, I was not ignorant of this. This was a database headquartered in London where *drinking and singing* seemed to match *strength and breath.* He was very concerned about this, however, as I could see it in his eyes. He wanted nothing to do with the operation I would undertake and feigned judgement, boredom and disconnection.

I am a woman who needs little convincing when it comes to jobs. I accepted the mission without question and put to one side what I thought about the man's sanity—Blake himself could teeter daily between rationality and lunacy. In my experience, however, there is little contrast between the two. I knew precisely how the database could be hacked and went about this in my way for 48 hours. I delivered the necessary data during this time and delivered it to Nakadai who, in turn, delivered it to Professor

> Mutton. The real *clothing of delight* came from *your* government, notwithstanding; they were the ones who bought me to influence your general election. I did this very well, I must say...

Tatyana was not noted for her faculties of introspection and so failed to mention that her hackish meddling resulted in a breakdown within London's mainframe. The mainframe, which operated similarly to the conductor *Sir Charles Groves*, controlled and regulated traffic lights, fully-automated public transport, water pumps, public elevators, air-conditioning and Wi-Fi. Tatyana's meddling forced the mainframe to ferociously collapse, however, and numerous brutal traffic accidents occurred, expensive and complex wiring was flooded as well as with busy tube lines, public elevators either plummeted or rocketed out of their shafts, air-conditioning short-circuited and Wi-Fi disappeared and sozzled hospital records as well as a minor destructive flux in the global stock market. The London Offline, therefore, was an unprecedented cataclysm and the equivalent of *Monteverdi*'s innovations which led to opera becoming a vehicle for dramatic expression.

I was teaching the three Modules of Death at the time and remember fielding questions about it. Little did I know, of course, that Nakadai had been involved with the whole event under duress. No one was more aware of this than Nakadai himself, however, and immeasurable guilt, forlorn penitence and remorse racked his brain for many months. He was sure that such tempestuous, sensorial sensations would continue to mark and determine his shaky decision-making to his dying day.

I was distressed by my schizophrenic involvement with the *London Offline*. That's what people called that awful day, and I was partly responsible. I was always in two minds about the Word Machine project. On the one hand, I hoped to be able to find the Perfect Word as described by Snül—but otherwise, the purpose of the Word Machine was malevolent and evil. In my calculating the Perfect Word I would summon up the Great Word; I would calculate my *destruction*. Maybe that is why the Japanese were so wary of Catholicism when it reached our shores. Over the years we have had secular materialism, social Darwinism, Marxism, Protestantism and what some referred to as the modern recalibration of Buddhism— but did those ideologies approach the all-encompassing characteristics of Christianity? Were they as *unafraid* as Christ? At the same time, Mutton called upon our first motive constantly. *The Perfect Word was in our grasp*, he would say, *and there was no way security would hinder our academic integrity.* That was what I lacked, though! I wanted security and integrity; I wanted to be safe. I was that contemporary man facing secularism and atheism. Where would my existential self-consciousness end up? Would I be able, as a religious person, to prevent myself from being harmed by these constants which in themselves were religious? I had a sense of regret most powerful: I allowed that Captain Khuhro nonsense to distract me from your work, Nicola; I had wronged my family

> and parents; I felt most sorry for Luka Graf and the senseless waste I inspired in him. I knew for sure I needed a holiday...

I had never seen a man so despairing and doleful—Nakadai seemed to lean upon his desolation as Lotte Lehmann's performance of Desdemona in Verdi's *Otello* leaned upon the destiny of a doomed woman. He turned to his second pair of hands as always, however, and showed Goro Saito his creation on an eerily surreptitious night.

> Professor Mutton tells me that he has access to my mind, these memoirish episodes, but I don't care anymore. Let him see...
>
> The problem, as far as I could see it, would be this—If I showed Goro the Word Machine, explained its basic principles and allowed him to glance at the raw linguistic matter that would be fed into the device he would ask me where I had found this raw linguistic matter in the first place. If I mentioned Tatyana, therefore, there was a possibility that Goro would mention Tatyana to somebody else. This, like the modification of Catholic celebration to appease local custom, was not an option. If it was, however, would I be able to silence Goro—and would our respective Japanese Bishops have the gall to stifle the *internal influence* of Japan's culture upon its revised form of Christianity?

The urges surrounding Goro were frightening. I had not experienced them since the Tsushima War, that is, the urge to kill and survive. His saving grace was his familiarity with my secrecy, and not answering questions. For example, I remember he asked me once if I would ever get married. Two years later, I found Goro in the staff toilets, and said, "No."

Regardless, the time came for Goro to pay a visit to my office, late at night, a printed portion of *raw linguistic matter* resting in his lap.

"Its subject is suspect," said Goro, like someone rejecting how one's parents were the originators of one's body and soul. "Good news is that it's opportunistic. I assume that that was intended when it was collected?"

"We've been focusing inwards for too long," I said, sidestepping his question. "Now is the time to be unfocused, to project outwards. Clearly, coherently, logically."

Goro shook his head. "Nakadai-san, I don't understand." *So much for sacramental grace*, I thought. "And what the hell is that thing?" he pointed at the Word Machine in the corner of the room.

I pulled a long wire from beneath my desk. It was connected to my desktop computer and I plugged it into the Word Machine.

"What does Mardik Snül say?" I allowed Goro, briefly, to bring the aforementioned Diacritic theorist to mind. "If there can be one word for any other word," I argued, "Then we can assume there can be one word for every word: an all-encompassing word that will make language redundant."

"Every junior linguist knows Snül's Maxims," Goro assured me. "That's first-year stuff, ground zero—I'm pooped, what time is it? Well, hold up...if that's the *aim* of the experiment—"

"What, tiring you out?"

"No, coming up with a perfect word, with a—with a—the aim of the experiment, creative or not, is to produce a perfect word. But, Nakadai-san, to do that you'd have to build—build a—oh my God, you clever bastard—you—you're going to calculate the perfect word? So, this is the Word Machine! You built it!"

"It's not Ikea, Goro." *Say what you will about Judas, but the man was party to the extraordinary*, I thought.

Judas Iscariot's surname, moreover, was most likely a slanderous alteration of *sicarius*—which is Latin for *murderer*. This gets even more complicated when you have in mind how the Spanish word *sicario* means *hitman* or *hired killer*. We might conclude here that the Catholic faith has never let the truth get in the way of a good story.

"But yes," I went on, "I'm finally going to calculate the perfect word—I mean, we are." I hunched over slightly, like an older parish vicar inspecting her wine supply. "The thing about large mechanical devices

> hiding in office corners is that they tend to have a tiny compartment...in those tiny compartments are usually either power cores or the core text used by dissenters from an older religious order. Ah, yes—"
>
> I opened a drawer in my desk. I removed the mallenium core which Smythe had so happily provided and installed it into the Word Machine. I closed the cavity and rubbed my hands together, then flicked a switch on the wall. The Word Machine's appendages began to snap and click. Goro's eyes lit up. "It's beautiful."
>
> "It's not beautiful," I said, "it's work..."

This work would culminate in what perhaps was the most upsetting event in the University of Twickley's history. It would be more damaging than the Higher Education Strike; more shattering than the Pedagogic Interregnum; more wounding than Offenbach's *Orpheus in the Underworld*; and more affecting than every song ever written in the *sonata form*. The power that Nakadai would tap would be alien—but he, as always, would be *all too human*.

15

ROTTEN EGG—LUMB—ACCOMPLICE—DAWN TOMORROW

In what proved to be one of the most duplicitous, uncanny and combustible deeds since *Columbia Records* dumped Johnny Cash, Goro Saito was invited to Zeta Palazzo's cottage to discuss Nakadai's potential for deception. Saito briefed Nakadai on what had happened the following day and much to Saito's apprehensive bewilderment he set himself the task of fictionalizing it in one of his memoirish philosophical fragments. This was the preliminary hacksaw that began to separate Saito and Nakadai. I have copied out the text in its entirety, however, and should like you, dear reader, to make up your mind.

> We have, as testified by Christ, this polarity between *word and deed*. There is a tension between the things we say and the things we do and how both pertain to our moral responsibility. Christ argues that between *word and deed* it is the latter that is more important. In other words, our actions have a

greater impact on our moral responsibility, and how we might exercise it.

One cold night, Goro walked up a tiny hill to a cottage surrounded by fields, sheep and frost. The truth was that Professor Zeta Palazzo owned the cottage, and she had asked Goro to visit her that evening

Inside Goro stared at the bag of *Heavy Gong Takeaway* food on the table in the centre of the snuggled room. Having smuggled a pocketful of luck in with him, Goro turned to Zeta and said, "What happened at the Christmas party last year...I'm sorry my bits didn't work...I get nervous, sometimes... I'm sorry..."

The brush-thick hair standing vertically on Zeta's skull bristled with annoyance. "I didn't bring you here for sex! Palazzo can find sex anywhere and anytime," she replied in the third person.

"Oh—that's nice," said Goro, his loins preparing themselves for a Biblical *war of aggression* more than anything else.

"You didn't leave your office all day. You must be tired—sit down, Goro. I always find it remarkable how hungry I am after thinking for a long time. Do you find that?"

"I keep a bowl of wasabi peas next to my laptop." Goro sat down. "I don't notice the sensation."

"Always thinking ahead. I like it." Zeta pulled out plastic containers packed with poorly-cooked Chinese food. They tucked into their respective dishes and basked in the asexually sexual tension.

After having her fill of tension and food, in the manner practiced by less stable Buddhist monks, Zeta rested her elbows on the table. "There is a rotten egg, Goro."

Her colleague ceased his mastication. "In the food?"

"No, you idiot! I mean our department! There is a snooper at the top of the faculty. He is doing illegals under our noses. Nobody is to know I have said these things. Nobody."

Goro swallowed a *jubilee's* worth of udon noodles. They belonged in Japanese and not Chinese food technically, but he approved westerners at least trying to be authentic—even if they overshot by 1,838 miles. Whether the Israelites, after their deliverance from Egypt, would have been open to ingesting copious amounts of udon noodles is something that distracted Goro from listening to Palazzo. "Why are you telling me this?"

"Any person who leaves an Anglo-Saxon boarding school after 19 years to become a lecturer at a university is a person I can trust," she argued. "You're like the owner of a café; you are not interested in comfort or money. Many would say you were, as a result, mentally challenged—but these are people who live in the false assumption that nothing is challenging about being intelligent. You're not stupid because I *know* you're not stupid. I trust you for the reasons I have already outlined. If we decide to trust this snooper, however, then we might as well trust God to shine his shoes..."

"Who is it?" asked Goro.

"One of 8 professors in our department."

The anger he expressed may have been an example of *bad faith*, but there was no doubting that Goro's conscience was addled by something. "You belong with the Pedagogical Interregnum sympathizers! You want to take us back to the dark ages! What do you think you're doing?"

"Calm down—"

"Don't tell me to calm down! I didn't come out here in the middle of the night just so you could toss conspiracy theories at me! You tell me to calm down when you've sidelined cause in favour of reaction?"

"This isn't one of your *Gamera* nights where you sneak into lecture rooms to indulge your childhood; this is serious—"

"That is confidential!" Goro raved.

"You're here because of an absolute conviction that there is something wrong with our department." An uncomfortable silence blossomed in the cottage. "It needs to be remedied as soon as possible. Because, in my capacity as the head of the Department of English Language & Linguistics at the University of Twickley, I am in control—do you understand me?"

She stood up walking across the living room. Then she parted her blinds. There was nothing but darkness outside because it was nighttime. She wondered why she had done this.

"Why not an assistant lecturer," Goro sounded rather desperate, "or a PhD student?"

"Don't be deluded." Zeta theatrically turned toward her colleague. "No academic in their right mind," and right-minded academics were suspect at the best of time, "would consciously sabotage up their career—"

"Until they got to the top and could get away with—well, they haven't murdered anyone, have they?"

"Thousands, Goro. The London Offline was an unparalleled nightmare. The thought of somebody hacking into the mainframe of a city that large, accidentally ceasing electricity for 3 hours and not sticking around to clear up the bodies with squidgies makes me sick."

"I fail to see what the London Offline has to do with the University of Twickley," said Goro.

"The snooper and the London Offline are connected. They're each a half of an angry, lopsided symbiosis. I see no reason to exert energy trying to convince you until you make that connection *yourself*."

"*Masaka*—"

"Don't talk in Japanese. I don't know what you're saying."

Goro lied and said, "I was just saying, I don't believe it."

Zeta returned to her seat. "My 8 suspects are myself..." (Goro rolled his eyes at this; he didn't see it as an act of modesty.) "Duni Mwangangi, Jenson Hewitt, Omar Braddock, Ronnie Combs, Ellis Mutton, Berretta Vecoli—and Nakadai, of course."

The helium had been escaped out of Goro's face by somebody way too preoccupied with fart sounds and their variations. This happened to vicars when they discussed *bigotry* for too long. "You can't be serious."

"I'm deadly serious."

"Nakadai? Come on, Zeta—"

"Do you know something I don't know, Goro?"

"No...I don't..."

Goro had seen the Word Machine and that was enough to get him into trouble. Though he didn't understand how the machine worked. Could it have caused the London Offline?

He floundered, "Nakadai is a workaholic. I don't see how he'd have time to come up with...*nefarious plans*."

"I have far more work to do than Nakadai," said Zeta proudly. "But I don't live a life that consists solely of my work." With her free hand, she touched Goro's and drank in the *book of common prayer* that was his skin. "If that were true, where would we find the time for the wild things *we* do...?"

With this text, Nakadai insinuated that Saito had been rogering Professor Palazzo and that the entire department would deviously double-cross him. I couldn't believe that Nakadai was capable of ransacking the depths of such immaturity, pettiness and unrefined, salacious gossip. It was like Krenek's experimentation (which led to the first jazz opera) had mated with Ice Cube's *No Vaseline*. All the same, it demonstrated how willing and able Palazzo was to commit Nakadai to the flames whilst Mutton, who was the real culprit, continued to flourish unharmed.

The situation grew much worse when, the following day, two policemen drove haphazardly onto campus and parked their shabby and worn-out car. They showed unflattering IDs to the porter and were directed to Arkham Main, towards which they targeted their investigative noses. They set off in a fashion which, had they been actors in a low-budget police drama, would have been accompanied by the slowly-building tempo of chugging taiko drums or the melancholic gaze of Mozart's *Jupiter Symphony*.

Nakadai watched the policemen, allegedly, making their way through Arkham Main where they intended to speak with Professor Mutton. Ever since the London Offline, the cogs of Anglo-Saxon justice had turned inexorably towards the University of Twickley. They had liaised with Japan's Second Intelligence Department who, having arrested Tatyana Baryshev, were torturously questioning her in a Japanese prison. Thus, as Nakadai watched the policemen strut their constabulary stuff, he concluded that whatever would follow would be tactless.

> I stalked them into the building. I recognized the more waspish of the two; the pockmarked man who stirred memories in me as though I had met him on a Japanese

beach in a previous life where I smuggled Portuguese missionaries. It was none other than DCI Lumb, who I had blinded in a precise moment of reactionary ferocity during the Higher Education Strike. I was ashamed of what I had done to his face, even though he would probably have killed me—and if not him, his subordinates would have killed me. I was lost for words, however, at our meeting again under such serpentine circumstances and I didn't look forward to his surveying me with one monotonous, penetrating eye. I followed them as they quickly made their way into the relevant hallway and knocked on Professor Mutton's door. They had none of that *sanguine temperament* we Catholics think so highly of; their manners were brutal when the ostensibly kindly Professor *Emeritus* opened the door. He was unusually cordial and prepared to dispatch them in the most effective way which mirrored their brutal natures. He asked them if they wouldn't mind discussing matters in a different room; to my horror, he showed them into *my* office which, as I had left it unlocked, presented the perfect coffin. Mutton saw me lurking at the end of the corridor like a man awaiting the *second coming of Christ.* "Hello, Nakadai!" he shouted. "Don't be afraid! They only want to ask us some questions!" I trudged sadly into the office and Mutton locked the door behind us. DCI Lumb spotted me through his lonely green eye when I entered the room, then evidently restrained himself. With my puny, revolting presence in the room, however, it would appear that I was as unlucky as Barrabas—forever sullied in the view of one angry, green eye. He asked, "What did you say your name was?" I told him my name and the black marble that packed his precarious right socket seemed to expand from the icy intention that was filling his decidedly corrupt brain. Then Mutton got between us: "You won't mind if I sidestep feeble jokes and the appropriate wintry smile?" he said coolly. "From what I can tell, your investigations boil down to this little device in the corner here. That's my confession. I hope you feel Augustine's *Confessions* to be the most important book ever written, as I do. There's no doubting that; but please *doubt* this device I'm pointing at. I know it looks innocent enough, but so did *The Critique of Pure Reason*. And like that book this machine's going to revolutionize everything. Yes, everything! That's *just* the type of work we do here, isn't that right, Nakadai? (I nodded shamefully.) But I'm afraid this machine was built by a malicious person, a Weininger, a Spengler, a Frege—all names you recognize, I'm sure...look behind it...you'll find what I say about its being revolutionary and evil to be *true*. The prime suspect. We must be careful, though. If you know anything about Broad's three theories of truth (correspondence, coherence and pragmatic) you'll know that you can't reduce philosophy to *theories*. Thus here, we can't reduce the danger to blind investigation. Now, if you will, I would suggest you help your deputy because it *is* quite heavy." DCI Lumb decided against indulging his rage and

> decided to do what Professor Mutton had so innocently and helpfully suggested. "Come on, Mike," he nodded at his sergeant; "Give us a hand." They ducked behind the Word Machine, made contact with its surface and were both shattered into crimson filaments of dust when, conveniently, Professor Mutton flicked a switch at my desktop computer. I discerned the dying men's skeletons and their decomposing red shapes—but their bodies soon disintegrated completely into dust and left my eyes bulging at the disgusting monstrosity that had just occurred; my nerves broken and my legs like jelly. This was where my *vow of obedience* had led me; the oath I would otherwise have taken under the Vatican Council I had instead taken under this *pretend* God who did not love human beings but wanted their reality...

It was clear that Mutton's vitality had resumed and he ordered Nakadai to take his brush and dustpan and sweep up the dead policemen's remains. He did so in stunned silence, akin to the break in Addinsell's *Warsaw Concerto*, and poured the ruby powder into a black bin bag. Nakadai tried to avoid getting the pulverized and claret-coloured substance on his trousers, but failed and found his thighs covered in dead people. Upset, he followed Mutton's orders to take the bag in his cobalt-blue Chevrolet to a quiet spot in the country and conspiratorially dispose of its corroded contents.

After an hour's drive Nakadai discovered what appeared to be an area free of human spectators. He drove under a layby canopied by branches connected to a pocket-sized dictionary of black trees. The circumstances were so extreme that Nakadai thought he had walked into one of Dame Myra Hess's wartime recitals in the National Gallery in London. There was a wind when Nakadai opened the boot of the car and emptied the bag's powdery contents onto the dead grass and moist rocks below. He folded the bin bag away and shakily returned his sweaty bottom to the driver's seat. To deceive passing cars, he drove with the light and delicate elegance heard in *rococo* music and arrived back at the University of Twickley where, regally lounging in the high-backed chair of his own office, Mutton declared to Nakadai that the influx of the Great Word would take place at dawn the following day.

Coincidentally the next morning would also see a departmental meeting chaired by Zeta Palazzo; a gathering in which Professor Hiroshi Nakadai would be charged with misleading colleagues, breaking university regulations and incontinently haemorrhaging salacious gossip. They would intend to determine Nakadai's future at this research establishment; though given Mutton's apocalyptic plans, the meeting itself would likely fade into history like Schubert's *Trout Quartet.*

16

DEPARTMENTAL—DUEL—DESTRUCTION

Nakadai was nowhere to be seen on the morning of Armageddon. The Department of English Language & Linguistics carried the meeting's agenda under their arms when they entered the colourless meeting room. The agenda, regardless of debate, was the liquidation of Nakadai's employment. The fly on the wall was Goro Saito, however, whose experience was recalled to Nakadai weeks later; and which I must now include in my recreation of what happened on that fateful day.

The meeting had been called to mull over Nakadai's professorship but Palazzo had seen to it that Nakadai would be nowhere near the meeting; nor would he be aware of its premeditated existence. It was like William Mathias being excommunicated from his Welsh heartland and prevented from teaching entirely. Verily, there was a nervous hubbub as a subdued Mutton entered the room and took a seat at the back of the room. Palazzo banged her fist on the table and stated the agenda which constituted an elucidation of demented particulars.

Dr. Ines Machado was most upset. "If we make Nakadai redundant, we need to suss out who'll do the washing-up in the restroom."

"I said at the beginning that I would show no mercy towards Nakadai, none whatsoever," Palazzo replied. "I don't know why you are *laughing*, Ines. I'm going to make sure he retires either today or tomorrow and that he is never again allowed to work at any research institution. I have contacts everywhere, as many of you know—it is also my *pleasure* and my *profession*. You are welcome to take issue with what I have said. However, if you do that, then I will take issue with *you*. Ladies and gentlemen, I am fed up and *tired* of Nakadai running circles around our regulation; our constitution. If he *were* a good man, he would have flown to Tibet after the year *he* has had—but he continues to roam these halls like some begrudged janitor."

Professor Mutton enjoyed the proceedings like some gradually-unfolding *adagio* composed by Tōru Takemitsu. "He should have gone back to Japan *years* ago," he whispered to Professor Vecoli.

"I'm sorry," Dr. Waller disagreed, "but Nakadai has turned down every offer from every other university. He's been head-hunted more times than Cornel West! He has been loyal and you can't *deny* that! I would go so far as to say that Nakadai loves this place; he loves us in his strange way."

"Martha, he doesn't know any different," Dr. Jeptoo said. "The man has been here his *whole* life; that can't be good, can it? I can't fathom why they kept him on for a PhD—"

"Because," Professor Braddock shouted, "he was brilliant! Because we needed money and Nakadai was an investor's dream—"

"You mean the *university* needed money?" Dr. Sweet was sore.

"We *are* the university."

Palazzo was unimpressed by the miasma of inessential discourse permeating the room. "He is embarrassing us by staying here. *That* is the crux of the matter."

Meanwhile Mutton had started clapping; like the one person who had gone to see Rossini's *Barber of Seville*, he was alone in his applause and gradually rose from his seat. "There is something of Wittgenstein's *viva voce* in this—it's quite absurd." His hair was brilliantly white and bristled with energy. The satin inscrutability of his diamond-like eyes had returned. "He was my tutee all those years ago—Nakadai, *not* Wittgenstein. Then again, who knows?" He paused. "I'm going to preface my decision with a disclaimer. I'm sure none of you expected that."

The academics in attendance were very confused.

"You're all trying to avoid my eyes. That's all you ever do, isn't it? You're disturbed by real philosophical reflection. You think it's fascism—it's probably more like Bolshevism."

"Get *on* with it," Palazzo complained.

"No one thought Bertrand Russell had any more work in him. They were right—but for those of you who think I'm done because I'm old...I'm *much* too old to care what you think. If you dislike what I think should be done with Nakadai, you will have to take it up with God. You'll all be meeting him soon anyway. *Thus, it pains me to say that it's best if Nakadai goes.* He is a shipwreck; he had such potential—but he is a shipwreck...*chop, chop...chop, chop*...you're all looking for the religion of the future, but you never think *not* to look between your legs."

There were embarrassed gasps. Some thought he had become senile.

Palazzo squinted. "I *beg* your pardon?"

"You're like Frege when he died: quite redundant," Mutton spoke. "You were always *particularly* irritating, Zeta; you always wanted to know what the point was before anything got published. Never minding your own business. All proper philosophy begins with a confession, so here's mine—*you have all been used*. Every last one of you. You've been used. You are pawns in a game you are too ignorant to understand. You have ears, though—can you hear it? The Word Machine *gurgling* away? The only time we're fresh in our thinking is when we change position and develop something new. We've entered the final stages of direct transference—you'll be wiped off the face of the earth! I'm going to make a better world, a better *word*, you could say!" He laughed and relished every moment. "You have *all* been used!"

Saito decidedly shook his head in disappointment and kicked himself for not staying at Cheltenham College. In the same way that every sacred work Anfossi composed was brilliant, he concluded that everything *had* to be Nakadai's fault.

In the meantime, Nakadai had called me to a certain seminar room downstairs where he had explained what was happening. I could sense something bad was happening in his office. A strange light emanated from across the court and through the window. Nakadai assured me that the stakes were as high as when Mozart composed his *Prussian Quartets* to please King Friedrich Wilhelm II—I expressly agreed with him.

"Here—we must wear these," said Nakadai as he handed me what appeared to be a circuit-covered bracelet. "It's kind of a psychic barrier. It will prevent that thing from getting into your head."

"Does it work?"

"Don't argue! Just wear it!"

The room started to shake when I put the bracelet on; there came a ghastly gurgling sound that enveloped each surface.

Nakadai stared deeply through his office window on the other side. The greater the colour, the more concerned he became. "I think it's about time I finished my confession," he said.

"What?"

"The broader picture."

The gurgling sound seemed to peak. We stared at one another when it fell again. "Why do I feel like that was an overload?" I asked.

"It's reached the final phase earlier than I thought! The mallenium core will burn out!"

"You mean we went all the way to Norway—"[1]

"Yes!" We ran out of the seminar room as though we were Communists who had mistakenly wandered into a performance of a Derek Bourgeois concerto. We sprinted over the trimmed grass in the courtyard, then up the stairs approaching our department.

He stopped briefly and emitted a set of whinny noises. "Nicola, you need to get everyone out of this building," he said. "It's much worse than I thought."

[1] See *Nakadai and the Nordic Menace.*

I surveyed the fire alarm on the wall. "I don't want to get prosecuted—"

"Smash it! Eghgthgjt!" He paused. "The Word Machine! It's destroying our language!"

"Gwethreigh. What am I saying?"

"Eghththp!"

I punched the glass and watched confused undergraduates wander outside. The alarm danced over the otherworldly gurgling as I ran through corridors telling people that a fire had started in Nakadai's office. "That doesn't surpplkn me," most people replied.

Nakadai pushed through screaming parcels of people as pandemonium unfolded in the department. He spotted that evil viridescent glow from the vicinity of his office and prepared himself something like the destiny *Imogen Holst* experienced when she organized the Aldeburgh Festival with Benjamin Britten; a friend of her planetary father.

The door, however, was charred. He kicked the door down with his feet and found Professor Mutton looking worried amongst Nakadai's melted belongings. He caught sight of Nakadai and glared passionately. "It was *I* who put the dogshit outside Egami's room! I admit it!" he declared vehemently.

Nakadai ignored this revelation and said that he had followed Mardik Snül's designs flawlessly. The truth, unfortunately, was that Snül and those before him had sabotaged the plans on purpose. "Cmnbdg?" Mutton replied. "What did I—?"

"Everyone that you have used has in turn been *fooling* you, Mutton! All along!"

He allowed *this* revelation to set in. Mutton slowly realized that every servant he had had on this long and unhappy path had been quietly working against him and the will of the Great Word. Then, like a high note played by Ruggiero Ricci on his violin on one of his Soviet Union tours, the great professor seemed to crack under his own failure to perceive.

"But we have got to get out of here!" Nakadai broke through. "It's going to wethumfn!"

"*Noomasd*," Mutton hissed and twisted his face in agony. "I won't let you tasfhnlnvdlkn! This is my saviour—this is my God! How could you possibly think of murdering a God? You're too wercnght! I mean—*you're too late, Nakadai!*"

There ensued brief fisticuffs with Nakadai trying to drag Mutton away. Despite this man's odious influence, he had a right to live; Nakadai was determined to practice forgiveness in the extreme. Mutton, fighting back as though he were John Taverner during his tenure as chorister-instructor at Cardinal College, pushed Nakadai through the smoking doorway.

I meanwhile had been watching the ramifications and reverberations of the Word Machine's pulsations across campus. A mainline filled with water had burst under the square sending freezing geysers up into the sky and coating fleeing students, academics, accountants and janitors. The gurgling which did not affect either Nakadai or me seemed alternatively to drive those of a conflicting mental disposition certifiably psychotic. There were people in the square who had begun emitting that very same whinnying that Nakadai had produced in the stairwell. I realized how these people were coming under the control of the geo-spatial demon which was worming its way through the Word Machine. These afflicted people who, broadly speaking, were students of literature and linguistics, ran in circles and brutishly attacked any foreign body that interrupted their path.

The police arrived like *canticles*: each one distinct but equally dogmatic. They were immediately attacked by these afflicted people. The windows on the library exploded and destroyed seating outside the *Student Union Shop*; the 200-year-old oak tree in Mutton College caught fire and then was extinguished by a brief spell of divinely inspired hail; the visiting *Mastersingers of Nuremberg* ran away from the steadily collapsing statue of Saint Xavier. Speaking as someone who saw it happen—everything pointed toward Armageddon!

I recognized that Nakadai had handled it, fortunately, when I spotted him running past the Department of Biological Sciences; his torn trousers and bloodied face spoke to his having listened to Debussy's *Syrinx* without wearing a helmet—but I knew the culprit could only have been Professor Mutton himself who, regrettably, was missing.

"Nakadai! Dkelldbsh!" I cried. He joined me at the edge of the university square and paused in dissatisfied trepidation when he saw that I was staring into the air. "Wtuo sgfh iteu?" he asked.

He turned to find what I found so captivating—which, as it turned out, was how the Arkham Main building had split in two. Half of the building was on the ground whilst the other half was floating and spinning in the air; trails of concrete, wood and plastic were suspended between the two halves. The light and the gurgling were pulsating and getting louder. Nakadai gripped my shoulder and said, "Ghetg dgjow!" as Arkham Main's levitating section exploded like an overworked lightbulb.

The veiny and viscous green colour that, for a time, had saturated the skies soon dissipated. The afflicted people in the square who had been strangling policemen stopped altogether and fell one by one to the cold ground. There came across Nakadai's face an expression that rested somewhere between sly malice and brief but intense gratitude—or so he would describe it whenever he told this story...

The general feeling was that we had reached the end of an especially tiring performance of Halévy's *La Juive*—but whilst there had been executions of the kind perpetrated by Cardinal di Brogni, there had been no malicious twist where, like di Brogni, we had found that those we had condemned to death had been our *own* children. Pockets of charred smoke danced in various regions across campus; it was refreshingly quiet and the faint hissing sound of escaping water permeated the atmosphere as birdsong, too, returned.

I brushed the dust and other charred materials from my shoulders. "I want to aim to submit next month."

Nakadai coughed. "Is that wise?"

"I'm going to die if I keep hanging around you."

"Like a locket on a chain, tutors cannot explain; they can but make more contrived your academic pain."

"Beckett?"

He sighed and said, "Nakadai..." He sucked his finger and stoically held it in the air. He nodded approvingly. "Do you understand what has been going on?"

"It's been a rather *Pathetic Sonata*."

"Once upon a time...the Great Word divinely touched a cleric called *Elias Moton*. The Great Word promised him incredible things; he promised to extend his life if he created the Word Machine. The technology didn't exist at that time, thankfully; Muton, or *Mutton* as we knew him, had to wait for the world to catch up with his ideas—even if they *weren't* his ideas."

We walked together towards the Garden of Tender Recollections. "So, Mardik Snül *didn't* start the Neo-Linguistic movement?"

"Certainly not," said Nakadai as we sat on the remaining bench. "Nor did Yågosh or Lippanánga. Mutton merely used them as a front whilst he did the real work behind the scenes; he used their ideas, though, because they had first-class brains, all of them..."

"Why did he need you, though?"

"How refreshing to have modesty foisted onto me," he said. "The Diacritics were all dead. Mutton wasn't clever enough to keep the work afloat. He needed someone new whilst the technology, slow as it was, caught up to where he needed it to be. I'll have you know that the Great Word was quite *fond* of me!"

In Donizetti's *Daughter of the Regiment* the Tyrolese peasant turns out to be the daughter of the Marquise de Birkenfeld. I couldn't help thinking that the same applied to Nakadai; that his parents were greater than he recognized—or knew, for that matter. (Had he been born to a virgin?)

"Where is Mutton?" I suddenly realized.

"He's gone."

"Gone? Gone where?"

"I am sure he's taken himself to hospital." Nakadai listened to the birds; I listened to the visiting *Mastersingers of Nuremberg* and their divine tuning. "He spent too much time around that machine at the critical stage—I warned him, but..."

"And the Great Word?"

He breathed in like Kathleen Ferrier used to. "The Great Word wanted the Word Machine. I *built* the Word Machine—then, due to an abounding trail of hand-me-down hypotheses, the Word Machine destroyed the Great Word. We worked together to defeat it. It's *quite* dead." He paused and looked around the rose garden. "Universities used to be lovely places. The name comes from the Latin *universitas*—it means *the whole*. Though, I doubt we could say we give people like you *the whole* at the best of times. Everything is in pieces now, and no one wants to put the puzzle together—assuming it *is* a puzzle." He cleared his throat and stood up. "There was a man called K.T. Fann who wrote a book called *Wittgenstein's Conception of Philosophy*. Then, after doing that he retired to Thailand and opened a bed and breakfast. I used to think that was stupid when I was young. Now though, I think he made a rather brilliant decision."

"You mean...you're going to *quit*?"

"Are you stark-raving mad? I love my job! I wouldn't change anything for the world. But there are those who *would*—and they must be stopped." He smiled. "But not today. *Start again.* Do you fancy a coffee?"

Nakadai and I ambled into Twickley and found an amenable café. He deposited his locomotive rapture into facial serenity. The smile that appeared on his face quelled seas and encouraged the undermined souls surrounding his robust frame. He blinked a few times and remembered the ground beneath his feet.

I now *end* my days by listening to Mozart's *Hunt Quartet*—that string quartet whose opening movement features a motif mimicking a hunting horn. I shower quickly, dress in my pyjamas and eat a fastidious supper of sausages and broccoli.

I stretch on the mattress I purchased from the half-price district of Twickley, then fall asleep with difficulty.

THE END

AUTHOR BIO

Walker Zupp was born in Bermuda in 1996. He has an MA in Creative Writing from Lancaster University. His first novel, *Martha*, was published by Montag Press in 2020.

Printed in Great Britain
by Amazon

84894237R00150